O! Enkidu!

The other story of
the Epic of Gilgamesh

Eric Farnsworth

Advanced Praise for O! Enkidu!

As hunter-gatherers weave between birdcalls and boulders, the city reaches for one wild young man. He enters its gate and gains a new self. Lucid and confident, this legend of love and betrayal moves us into its dream-flight. Desire has a ritual; grief, a flavor; determination, a knife.

— Tucker Lieberman, author of *Enkidu Is Dead and Not Dead / Enkidu está muerto y no lo está*

Eric Farnsworth shows us the *Epic of Gilgamesh* on a human scale through Enkidu's story, illuminating the foundations of our current world to suggest what we might create instead. Superb and highly original, *O! Enkidu!* is a conversational and poetic page-turner that will stay with you long after the last page.

— Caryn Mirriam-Goldberg, past Kansas Poet Laureate and author of *The Magic Eye*

O! Enkidu!

The other story of
the Epic of Gilgamesh

Eric Farnsworth

ISBN (perfect): 978-10159-524-00
ISBN (hardcover): 978-10159-524-17
ISBN (epub): 978-10159-524-24

First printed July, 2025
by Sphinx
(an imprint of Sul Books, LTD)
Lewes, UK / Rodenbourg, LUX

Cover and Interior Design: Sul Books
Cover Image: Mike Yoder, Eric Farnsworth

Find our books at SULBOOKS.COM

ONE

— I —

Enkidu frolics with the gazelle. See him silhouetted on the hill-side, leaping over the nabk bushes, his curly black hair streaming out behind him.

Meanwhile, down in Uruk, Gilgamesh rapes another virgin bride. For him it's just another tyrant workday, he scarcely notices. Where is Gilgamesh's mother when he does this kind of thing?

Little wonder, then, that the men of Uruk use the priestesses of Inanna to take the edge off their longing — after they have cashed in their grain crop with the priests.

But what of Enkidu out there in the wilderness? Surely he gets hungry sometimes. We can imagine him curling up with the foxes to sleep, but what does he eat? Does a wild man use fire to cook his dinner?

We picture ourselves hunting the gazelle. Roasting them, savory over a campfire. But could Enkidu really be frolicking with the gazelle and then be eating them too?

I'm wondering about Enkidu's mother now, too. Not to mention his father and sisters and brothers and cousins. Enkidu must have had a family — parents, anyway.

And what about the women of Uruk, now that I think of it? There is very little written about them. It seems that nearly all the scribes are men.

Once upon a time, there lived a man, Enkidu.

The Sumerians and Akkadians called him the Wild Man. Of course, by this, they tell us more about themselves than about Enkidu. But maybe they can tell us a little about Enkidu, too, if we look in the right places. Where do we start?

It would be good to begin our story at the beginning, but that is not possible. Only Enkidu's parents know where he was born, and they are lost to us.

But Enkidu's birth isn't really where the story begins, anyway. It starts much deeper in the past than even Sumeria. Did it start when we first tamed fire and made tools? Or when we spoke our first words or sang our first songs?

Or when we first danced with each other, saw ourselves dancing, and spoke a name for it?

These are all good beginnings, but they are hidden from us too, obscured by the haze of time.

We will need to start our story in the middle.

⸙⟐◇

Sîn-lēqi-unninni the scribe tells us that a young trapper living on the far fringes of Uruk spied Enkidu one day on the plains, running with the gazelle.

Enkidu was a wild man, hairy and naked, eating grass alongside the animals. The young trapper was frightened by Enkidu, by his great strength and savage appearance.

The trapper ran to tell his father, saying that the wild man had broken his snares, filled in his pitfalls and set the captured animals free. The father advised his son to go to Uruk to tell the story to Gilgamesh the king.

Gilgamesh heard the story and ordered that Shamhat the harlot of Inanna go to the hinterlands and seduce Enkidu. Shamhat should use her beauty and feminine charms, and thus render him tame.

Shamhat went with the trapper's son; she waited by a water hole for two days. When finally Enkidu came there, she dropped her robe and showed him her nakedness. Enkidu was bedazzled by her beauty.

They had sex for six days and seven nights. When Enkidu finally felt like going back to running with the gazelle, he was weak and smelled funny and the gazelle ran away without him. What was he to do but go back to Uruk with Shamhat?

No, let's start the story again.

The earth is moving. Since the glaciers have receded, there is no longer the great mass of ice pressing down on the land, and the land is rising up. The ice melts from the mountains in the north and the water flows to the lowlands, making a vast marsh seeping southward to the gulf.

The ground keeps rising, draining off some of the water cover, and a large wedge of land is becoming less marshy. This wedge lies between two rivers, one on the east and one to the west.

For many years, people had lived in small settlements around the edges of the lowland marsh, making their living from the abundance of plants and animals there. As the marsh dries and becomes more habitable, some of those people move across the rivers to the land between.

The new land is fertile, and the people are increasing in number. They are building larger settlements and this means they must find new ways of living with each other.

To the west of the western river, the one we call Euphrates, the land rises in sloping plains and low hills. These are furrowed by creeks that run freely in the cool wet season and then shrink to pools in the summer.

The plains and uplands grow thick with grass, green in the spring, and turn to gold in the dry season. The valleys support plum thickets and oak groves and the occasional reedy wetland. This land is not so fecund as the marshland between the rivers, its richness blooms and fades in cycle with the seasons.

Farther to the northwest are forested mountains.

Farther to the southwest the land turns to desert.

Enkidu and his family live in these borderlands, among the people who have not settled into permanent dwellings. They follow the herds of gazelle that roam the grasslands, continuing the old ways of many generations before them.

Along their annual circuit, they tell the stories and sing the songs that hold their memories to the land. At each place along their way, it is like greeting their friends or family. The children repeat the songs: here is where the plums grow, and here are the pistachios; now it is time to collect onions, and now the marsh reed roots.

As they travel they say the names for the edible plants and the medicinal plants and the poisonous plants whose places they pass. Their stories tell how the plants came to be in their places and how all the families and clans of plants and animals are related to each other.

Their songs draw pictures of what kind of place the plants choose for their homes, each according to their kind, and the people drop some seeds in fitting new places when they find them.

With the passage of time, they find more and better varieties of the plants that they use, such as the patches of barley and the clumps of sesame next to the stones where they do their grinding, or the berry bushes growing around the places where they relieve themselves.

Their circuit also takes them to the places where they collect the materials to make their clothing and their medicines, their baskets and their arrows, and their bows and their ceremonial preparations.

They keep some sheep, and perhaps a few goats, for milk and meat and wool and leather, and those animals mostly fend for themselves.

There are meeting places on the way where travelers come, and they swap stories or trade for arrowheads and knives made of obsidian from the mountains far to the north.

Depending on the weather and the quality of game and forage, the small nomadic band that is Enkidu's family will meet up with other family groups at certain times and places. There, they socialize and feast and perform the rituals of the seasons. There, they exchange the news from their travels, share their supplies, and arrange for new marriages.

The last few years have been harder for the nomads across the region. The weather has been warming, and the lush grasslands are shrinking. Everyone knows what this means. They can't afford to stay in any one place for as long as they once did, and when they move, they need to walk a little farther.

Young women are becoming less inclined to leave the security of their mothers' tents, and young men are less sure that they can get enough meat to feed a new family. And the married couples are taking more time between each new baby.

But the weather isn't the worst of it. The cities between the rivers are hungry and growing. They are taking the best land and ruining it with a plow. The city farmers are digging ditches, draining the wetlands, and diverting the river for their crops.

They stake out boundaries, then shout and swing sticks at anyone who tries to get to places that were once held in common. The farmers have stolen water holes and plum thickets and the marshes that once teemed with good reed tubers and fat ducks. The farmers burn the fields so that nothing grows but their grain and their cattle eat everything else. With all their toil, they are taking the fertility of the land, hoarding it, and using it up.

They seem to have forgotten that the land will give freely all that anyone needs, if only they give thanks in return, and don't take too much.

And some of the city people make a new child every year.

Roaming out beyond the fringe of city settlers, there are gangs of men who carry bronze weapons. These men do no useful work, but take what others produce, raiding both the outlying farmers and the nomadic bands. They kidnap young women to sell in the cities as slaves.

The most successful of these brigands have moved into the cities. They have bribed and threatened the temple priests who run the cities, taking political power and calling themselves "king." They have brought their henchmen with them and call them "army."

These kings amuse themselves with hunting parties, killing animals just for fun. They have wiped out the game animals near the cities, so they venture further and further into the wild lands looking for slaughter.

They don't even want the game, they just waste animals and call it "sport." Killing each one they can, even suckling mother, or younger than yearling, they take only the prize parts and leave the majority of the meat to the vultures and jackals.

In the days before, the good fertile land seemed endless, supporting the old way of living for more generations than anyone could count. But now the land is shrinking, getting swallowed by the cities, driving the nomads out to the scrub-lands and thorns.

How to make sense of the way those city people live? The nomads pass stories from the few among them who have spent time in the cities. The kings are wealthy beyond belief, yet they seem to always be grasping for more.

The priests have grown rich, they wear fine clothing and eat delicate food, and they wield power over the common people. Those who follow after the kings and priests, who style themselves aristocrats, can make things go badly for any ordinary person who might oppose them.

The soldiers swagger and take whatever they want, doing violence out of drunkenness, or habit, or for no reason at all. Every one of those people has gotten rich by taking from the farmers and herders and laborers, but what do those powerful people give in return?

The cities require the work of many artisans. Some of them are remarkably skillful and make useful things of incredible beauty. But most of the artisans take no care for their craft, quickly throwing together piles of shoddy things that will soon get tossed on a refuse heap. And the main share of the people — those who feed and clothe and build the city — look miserable most of the time. They are small and sickly, and their clothing wilts on them.

Even the ones who live to full adulthood are worn out by the time they have grandchildren. They only perk up during the festivals when the beer is flowing freely.

It isn't difficult for Enkidu's family to know what is happening. Even from the distance, they can smell it on the wind. It's no wonder that some people would try to leave the city and join up with the nomads.

There had been times when some of the nomad bands tried accepting people who escaped from the city — such is the normal custom of hospitality. But those city people were so different they almost seemed like another species.

They didn't have the skills they needed: they would look at the signs on the ground and still not see. Even if they took the time to learn, they were still foreigners. They talked too loud, their feet had no sense, they were always in the way, they never knew what anyone was thinking, and they didn't understand the jokes.

— 3 —

Enkidu is a big, hairy man. He is bigger and hairier than all the rest of his big, hairy family. The other nomad families call them "don't need a sheepskin."

And they don't need sheepskins. Of course, for most of the year, nobody else needs sheepskins either, especially with the weather as warm as it has been.

But look at Enkidu now, sitting silent at the edge of the marsh, staring at the reeds with his chin on his knees.

This is not like him.

It is the full moon just before the summer solstice, and the bush apricots are ripening. The best of the apricot thickets grows alongside a creek that waters a basket reed marshland. This is a customary place for one of their seasonal meetings.

When Enkidu and his family arrived at the meeting place, Enkidu's sweetheart wasn't there.

Her mother and her father, and her mother's mother, and father's mother, and father's father, and her older sister, and her older sister's husband, and her older sister's baby, and her two younger brothers, and the various aunts and uncles and cousins that Enkidu isn't in the mood to name right now, were all there.

But his sweetheart wasn't there.

Enkidu and Ninsigal were going to be married. Their people's customs don't require love to make a marriage, or vice versa, but it is good and lucky to have both. Enkidu and Ninsigal had been both good and lucky so far. Their families were in accord, and the couple had planned to pitch their own tent after this seasonal meeting.

But we must remember that Enkidu is really quite young.

He hasn't had time to get accustomed to heartbreak.

The nomads don't put numbers on years so we cannot be certain, but the year he was born was also the year his mother died. There were more soldiers than usual on the plains by the river that year, and Enkidu's family had to stay in the foothills for the dry season.

But Enkidu had no memory of losing his mother, and his aunts and grandparents doted on him. Enkidu's mother's sister had a baby girl only a month older than Enkidu, so she wrapped the baby who was nursing in her shawl while Enkidu's father's brother's wife held the baby who was sleeping. Passing from hand to hand when either got hungry or restless, the children each had two mothers, and when they started talking, they called each other 'twin.'

Enkidu was a happy child, quick to laugh, and he could run. His friend Ninsigal was about his age, agile, and she would run with him.

Enkidu could run fast and invisible through the tall grasses. Or mimic any bird call he heard, or pick a full basket of barberries without losing patience.

Ninsigal could follow him where he ran because she knew which way he would turn.

Usually, his twin sister kept close to their mothers. Sometimes Enkidu would come back from running and sit down with his sister and their mothers, helping with the weaving. When Ninsigal's family camped with Enkidu's, she would sit with them, the three of them together, combing wool or beating stalks of flax. Sometimes Ninsigal joined Enkidu and the other boys as they played their rough games, but often when the boys tumbled away to another adventure, she could be seen sitting there quietly, watching the crawling bugs climb back out of their holes, or collecting piles of pebbles by their color, red and yellow-white.

And later, people noticed Ninsigal's own ways, how she wove songbird breast feathers, soft and pale, into her shawl. Or how she fletched arrows using only crow feathers to match the black obsidian arrowheads.

Enkidu grew up big. The older boys from other clans might challenge him, but Enkidu would take it as a game. He'd wrestle them to the ground, then pick them up, slap their backs, and laugh. Though he had to learn to be careful. While he was having fun, sometimes those other boys might get angry.

After they joined their initiation groups, Enkidu and Ninsigal didn't see much of each other. The girls went with grandmothers and the boys with grandfathers.

They learned the old secrets, the mysteries of men and women filling up their days and nights, each in a camp off to itself. Breathing in the old stories with the smoke from their fires.

Then, after the months of initiation, when they came back, walking behind their grandparents into the main camps, the young men and women had become new people. Enkidu was yet bigger, sunburned, and muscled, and the hair on his face had grown thick and dark.

Coming into their camp one day, he was surprised to notice Ninsigal, now with breasts and hips and more of a quiet about her. They reintroduced themselves as if they were strangers, speaking politely with low voices, in the company of their adult relatives.

Talking with this new woman Ninsigal, Enkidu tilts his head. Sometimes he catches a glimpse of his old friend Ninsigal, but still, he wonders. His people are accustomed to knowing what is on the minds of their close companions, but with Ninsigal the source of the spring is deep out of sight. What wonders might come rising up from those depths? Of course, his sister has changed too, but she is still his sister. Standing next to her, he looks at Ninsigal, then nods a question to his sister. She just smiles and tells him, "Just wait, you'll see."

As time passes Enkidu and Ninsigal come to re-know each other, and it begins to feel natural for them to be alone together. Enkidu is learning to tell his jokes a different way — break them in the middle, and stack up the pieces, make a little fire with them so Ninsigal will laugh.

They are walking one evening along the brow of a hill, the grassland stretching below them making waves in the wind, running shadows in the lowering yellow light. The sun flares in their eyes, the sky goes flat and bright, the swifts swooping high in the air turn to silhouettes, and the grass below becomes dark and endless.

Enkidu takes Ninsigal's hand and feels body heat at her wrist where it presses against his. Her warmth spreads up his arm and across his chest and they are both floating above the grass with their eyes filled with light and their bodies as wide as the horizon.

Enkidu is about to laugh aloud, when he looks over to Ninsigal, steady beside him, calm like she's been here before.

She is still strong. She is still tall and she can still run.

Enkidu is a large man-boy like the rest of his cousins.

Ninsigal speaks more softly now, a little more distant, slower to laugh at a joke.

He knows what he wants; everyone knows. She knows it too, and she knows how she wants it. She lifts Enkidu's hand to her cheek so their lips won't spark the first time they kiss.

She has him go slowly. Use an easy touch — this isn't wrestling.

It is a new way for him, strength without force. So many things fill their senses as they pay close attention. The whole world of their bodies opens out in front of them.

— 4 —

No one was surprised that Enkidu came early to his manhood. Nor that he was about to marry the first woman that he loved. The path of his life had been untroubled, it fit him like well-made leather footwear — until today when he arrived at the bush apricot meeting and all of that was ripped apart.

At the last new moon, while he was traveling with his family he'd had a foreboding dream of Ninsigal taken away. In the dream there was a very large bird, it swooped down from the sky to catch her. Its legs spanned Ninsigal's shoulders, its talons clutching into her armpits. It caught her and lifted her up.

The great black wings swept clouds of dust up from the ground as the bird took Ninsigal away into the air. Enkidu was there and ran after them through the dust. The dust got in his eyes and he squinted his eyes open to not lose sight of Ninsigal, but, even so, the bird flew higher and higher, getting smaller in the distance.

Enkidu has been troubled ever since he woke from that dream. He was in a hurry to meet Ninsigal and put his mind at ease.

Enkidu's family band came into the meeting grounds as the evening light was falling, and they joined Ninsigal's family at their fire, each making their greetings in turn. Ninsigal's mother brought them fresh apricots and roasted hare with burnt apricot seeds. But where is Ninsigal?

They sit around the fire, leaning in so they can all hear and see while her father tells the story.

The family had been in the seed-grass hills, about eight days to the southeast, and Ninsigal went to check her grouse snares one day. When the evening came she hadn't returned.

This wasn't like her, so the next morning they followed her trail, and they found a disturbed place with donkey hoof prints, sandal prints, donkey droppings, and broken shrubbery like there had been a fight.

But they didn't find Ninsigal.

They followed the hoof prints for a day and into the next afternoon, but there came a windstorm blowing dust that erased all the traces.

"We were getting closer to them, but they were moving at a fair trot. We looked around for three more days but we never again picked up their signs. I can show you the hill where we lost them. Up until then, their trail was headed to Uruk."

Enkidu and his father and his older brother and his mother's brother and the men in Ninsigal's family stand up, swaying by the fire. They each wail a single note, pounding their chests between breaths. Enkidu's brother's wife and his father's brother's wife and all the women keen a high-pitched harmony as they stamp their feet on the ground.

Other people come from their fires nearby and join in the chorus. The voices swell together and raise a mass of air that quavers and thickens.

Enkidu feels the vibration expanding his chest. The air is getting denser, nearly liquid, and the weight of it fills his lungs. His body is getting heavier and larger; now he is looking down at the campfire from higher above.

He bends forward, reaching down to the fire, pulls a stick from the flames, and brings the glowing end to his waist. He scorches the knot that ties his plaited grass skirt. He drops the stick back into the fire, breaks the burnt knot, and pulls his skirt from his hips, rolling it into a bundle. A flight of sparks when he drops his skirt into the fire.

Enkidu turns to his father and they clasp arms, hands to biceps. Enkidu is still getting heavier. He releases his father and stumbles away from the fire down to the reedy marsh by the creek.

Sitting in a hand-breadth of water, he scoops up lumps of silty marsh mud and pastes it on his head and his shoulders and his chest and his groin.

Then he slumps flat to his back. There is the sky, straight up above him, out beyond marsh reeds. The stars are dimmed by the moon, but they look the same as they always do, just like last night and the night before.

The grief song voices get drowned by the water in his ears. The air smells of sulfur swamp rot.

When they find Enkidu the next morning curled up in the mud beside the marsh, nobody disturbs him. In the evening, when his father's brother's wife comes upon him still sitting there, she gives him a roasted fish. His father and uncle squat close beside him as he eats.

Days pass and Enkidu wanders the meeting grounds. Everyone there knows him, his closest relations take him in their arms. All of them put their hands on him, and they wait for Enkidu to speak first. But he doesn't speak.

This isn't normal, though no one could really be surprised.

It's strange to see Enkidu at the meeting not laughing and swapping stories. Instead, they see him sitting beside the goats and stroking their heads as they lie down to chew their cud.

Then time comes to break camp and move on. Enkidu's father kneels in front of him, holding his wrists and looking him in the eyes. It is time to go and they both know it. With the eyes, his father is begging Enkidu to pick himself up and come with them, but Enkidu doesn't get up.

Enkidu takes his father's hand and brings it toward him, pressing it to his chest. They can feel his heart beating. Enkidu presses his hand to his father's chest. They are both still alive.

Enkidu's older brother and his mother's brother come too and beg him to come with them. His brother's wife and his mother's brother's wife and his sister each hug him goodbye. The family is leaving now. Enkidu's brother's wife takes his hand and hooks the fingers around a woven bag that she has filled with dried meat. His sister holds onto him like she won't let go. She looks into his eyes and his eyes see her, and the eyes are full but don't speak. The family is leaving now, and finally, his sister kisses him and turns to go.

All of them have understood each other.

Enkidu loves his family. He doesn't want to part from them. But he has lost the power to go. He makes it clear that they will have to leave him.

He is sorry to disappoint them.

There is something that has stuck him to this place.

Day and night Enkidu sits with his chin on his knees.

The light changes and the wind bends the reeds.

At night it gets dark. The stars remain the same, but they are moving.

After a while it gets light.

On a morning, Enkidu stands. He turns away from the swampy water and starts to walk.

He is facing in the direction of Uruk.

— 5 —

Walking.

Putting one foot in front of the other.

Repeatedly.

Moving is better than not moving.

There is a rhythm to it.

Enkidu hasn't decided where he is walking, only to walk. To choose a destination requires something he lacks, but walking is good. The parts of his body that do the walking also do the deciding, if there is any deciding being done. In any case, it feels better to walk.

He walks all day. There is nothing else to do. He walks at night if there is moonlight to show a path. He sleeps beside the trail when he can't walk anymore.

He dropped the woven bag when the dried meat was finished.

He hasn't replaced his grass skirt.

He carries only himself.

⬩⧉⬦

At first, he followed the animal pathways, but he is getting closer to the city and the wild things have turned aside, circling back to their home places.

Here the ways all belong to humans. He has passed by the people's fields and their dwellings and the paddocks where they keep the animals they have tamed. He has bent down to drink water from the channels. They have tamed the water, too.

The birds are different here, chirping a strange language. His feet are crusted with cow manure and dirt from the roadway.

Now, whichever direction he looks, there are more people. Everywhere he sees their doing. There are people working their fields with mattocks and hoes. He sees women carrying baskets of soil on their heads.

The people watch him pass by, but they don't speak to him. As if he were not a man, only just some movement that distracts from their work day.

The air is filled with smoke and manure and fermentation and some acrid mineral smell. The wind makes no sense: it is carrying too many things. When people on the road come toward him, he stands aside but doesn't hide. They don't greet him and he doesn't menace. They see a big naked man and hurry on their way.

Finally, in the distance, he sees the walls of Uruk.

His sleeping mind stirs and begins to wonder. What violence these people must suffer to build such a massive defense? Or maybe it's not their lives. Maybe it's their possessions they are protecting.

So many possessions they must have! So many enemies coming here to raid them! He can't imagine what could be so highly prized to require such a wall. Clearly, to build a wall this massive took the labor of many men's lifetimes.

Only at this point does he pause to consider where he is going. He has been following his feet and this is where they have brought him. There is a hollow in his chest telling him that the city is entirely strange to him. Doubtless, it is full of people and customs and dangers that he knows nothing about. There is no way he could predict what might happen if he continues forward.

The moment passes, and his feet resume walking.

Here in front of him is the great river blocking the path to the city. He sees men with boats going back and forth across the river, carrying people and animals and produce from the farms. The passengers speak with the men in the boats. They are bargaining. These boatmen require some kind of payment before they will pole their boats across the river.

Enkidu pushes through the reeds at the river edge, steps into the water, and swims to the other side. The river is muddy, and the water tastes of too many animals too close together, but it is cool and smooth on his body.

He reaches the far bank and stands in the sun at the edge of the reeds beside the river, feeling the water from his hair drip down the backs of his legs. Standing there drying, his hands tucked into his armpits, he looks back across the river at the way he has come.

Not so wet now, he turns and parts through the reeds, back onto the road, and approaches the city gate. It looks as if his feet will carry him through it. As he gets nearer, he watches people come and go and crowd around the gate.

There are soldiers.

Richly dressed men are stopping people who pass through the gate. Soldiers block the people's way as the rich men look through the things people carry. Sometimes the rich men take things from the people. Sometimes they give them back.

Some of the people who are sitting by the gate are dressed in rags. Others are playing musical instruments. As Enkidu moves into the shadow of the city wall, everyone stops what they are doing and they stare at him.

A pair of soldiers step into the roadway and stand themselves in front of him, shouting in their language. One has a long bronze knife hung from his belt. The other holds a wooden pole topped with a bronze spear point. A question and a threat — the soldier shakes his spear as punctuation. Enkidu stands still, he doesn't know their answer and cannot give them what they want.

Some of the richly dressed men call out to the soldiers and begin walking toward them. They point at Enkidu and speak amongst themselves. A crowd has circled around him; most of the people look short and slow on their feet.

Enkidu can smell the fear on their breath.

The rich men finish their consultation, and two of them step away from the others and begin walking through the gate. One motions to the soldiers, and the soldiers push Enkidu to follow them. This is what his feet were waiting for, so he doesn't resist.

Inside the fortification now, he can see what these people are protecting. There are mud brick houses stacked on top of each other, many people going in and out of them. The people are busy, going here and there. They have many possessions. Some they carry. Some are laid out for trading.

He sees things made of leather and bronze and clay and all manner of fibers. There are baskets of produce, cucumbers and onions. Many rows of tall clay jars. Animals both killed and alive. The small children are busy too, chasing quick-running ducks, or picking pebbles from baskets of beans.

There are cook fires in clay ovens and clay bowls broken on the ground. The street is just as dusty inside the gate as outside, but here the dust is a little darker, with more bodies to color it.

The men are taking Enkidu down a wide street toward the middle of the city. The ground is packed clay, dead. Branching to the side he sees smaller lanes with more mud brick houses stacked up. There are more people going in and out.

A large structure is visible up ahead and they are moving toward it. As they continue, the houses alongside the street have been getting bigger, and the people around them are more finely dressed.

Here the pair of rich men leading them loosen their shoulders and walk a little easier. The houses are larger now but fewer people go in and out. The walls of the houses have been coated white, some painted with pictures.

The large structure ahead is set in a grand plaza. Workmen are carrying materials to new buildings along one side of the square.

Everywhere there are donkeys and carts and sheep and baskets of farm produce and grain. The dust and the smell of all the bodies remind Enkidu of how his people know when it is time to move on and make a new camp.

The walls enclosing the plaza are decorated with patterns made from small red and white and yellow tiles. Angled stripes of colored tiles set into mud brick. The patterns cover such a large area! They have made so many tiles!

The soldiers push through the crowd toward a building set a few steps up from the plaza, hustling Enkidu up the stairs past the crowds to stop at an arched doorway. As he stands behind the pair of rich men, Enkidu sees an old man and woman standing inside the doorway facing them, both draped with fabric made of impossibly fine thread.

Even this place seems to be on the way he is going. He doesn't need to fight them yet. The rich men tell a story to the old man and woman, then step aside and wait. In low voices, the old man and woman consult with each other, nodding as they speak, like a pair of herons.

A young messenger runs down the steps and disappears into the crowded plaza. When the messenger returns, the old man and woman nod again and turn back to the pair of rich men. They look at Enkidu, and then point to one of the new buildings. The rich men and soldiers take Enkidu that way. This was the right outcome.

They arrive at a pair of doors standing almost double Enkidu's height. The doors are hewn from cedar wood and hung on bronze hinges. The doorway of the building is faced with pale polished limestone. In front of the doors are two men wearing skirts of lion skin, Both of them are bigger but softer than the soldiers.

Enkidu feels a shiver at the small of his back.

He is confident that he could beat these two men, but they aren't giving off any human feelings.

The soldiers push Enkidu forward past the pair of rich men, and the lion-clad eunuchs nod their heads and open the doors.

Enkidu steps in, and the eunuchs close the doors behind him.

His eyes adjust to the dark of the room just in time to see a young naked backside hurry around a far corner. The floor is the same limestone as the outside doorway. The walls and ceiling are plastered. The only light is from two small openings above the doors. Enkidu has almost decided to follow the quick child when he sees his destination in front of him.

— 6 —

There is a woman facing Enkidu a few paces away. The woman is not Ninsigal, her hands have never skinned a gazelle. Even so, he feels a sensation of having arrived somewhere. She stands with her hands open as if to welcome him.

She is older than Ninsigal, fully curved under her fine linen draping. Her eyes are dark and don't seem to show any malice. Nor are they giving away any secrets. Enkidu can see that she knows many things.

She comes toward him slowly and calmly takes one of his hands in hers. She bends forward and kisses his face, just like she is his brother. The quick young boy has reappeared with a tray. The woman turns toward the boy and takes the tray with her free hand.

She leads Enkidu to a low platform covered with a plaited reed mat. Meanwhile, she is speaking softly in her language. As he watches her lips, Enkidu believes he can understand her.

They recline on the mat and she passes him a large cup of water. He hadn't known how thirsty he was. She refills the cup and he drains it again. He watches her long tapered fingers as she begins feeding him figs and dates and spoonfuls of a smoky pigeon stew. The boy returns with another tray, thick grainy beer and barley-spelt bread with honey.

It was then that Enkidu remembered he was naked.

The woman had seen him the whole time.

And thus we reach this place in our story.

The end of

the beginning of

the middle.

TWO

— I —

The woman was Shamhat, one of the chief Ladies of the Temple to Inanna at Uruk. There are reasons her name was remembered by Sîn-lēqi-unninni the scribe when he wrote his account more than a thousand years later. Some of what the scribe said about Shamhat and Enkidu is true, even though he garbled the story.

First, Shamhat tended to Enkidu's body. This was his first need, if not the greatest. She fed him, bathed him, and rubbed oil on his cracked feet. The boy brings fruits and bread and savory dishes and beer. Shamhat sees to Enkidu's education herself.

Thus, Enkidu has come to live in a room with walls and a doorway and a small courtyard beyond. There are three other doors from the courtyard opening to other rooms just like his, but with nobody in them. The walls are of brick, plastered white to reflect the light coming in from the sky above the courtyard. In the center of the courtyard is a pool, large enough to fit Enkidu's whole body in the water. In his room is a sleeping platform with a reed mat, and a pitcher of water.

The first night after he'd arrived in Shamhat's reception room at the temple, Enkidu fell into a sleep without sense, overcome by thirst and weariness from walking, rich food and beer, and the attention of a woman. In the morning when he finally awakes, she is there sitting beside him. She pours him a cup of water and keeps filling it until he is done drinking. He watches her eyes, he can feel her seeing him. She has painted a fine black line just above her eyelashes.

Then, lifting his hand, she gets him up from the sleeping platform and leads him down a corridor. As she walks with him, she is also speaking in her language. Telling him what she is doing and which way he should go. Enkidu hears a sound that draws his eyes from watching the curve of her cheek. Following down the nape of her neck, to shoulder, breast, waist, and hip, he sees the light fabric of her wrap make a swish as it slides on her smooth lower calf.

She leads him through a doorway to her private bath, lets go of his hand to slip out of her linen wrap, then steps into the warm bathing pool, turns to face him, and motions for him to come in.

Shamhat is as tall as many of the men in the city, even when she takes the silver clip from her plait and lets down her hair. It is fine and wavy black, not like Enkidu's coarse curly black. Her collar bones make a faint shadow above the curve of her breast, shoulders nearly as wide as her hips, the fullness of her thigh and calf traced with muscle as they flex, and her narrow heels widen to long toes. Her skin would be darker, but it seldom sees the full sun.

She doesn't shy away as Enkidu stares at her. He wants to see all of her at once, together with each of her parts. There is so much to look at, but she keeps moving around.

She dunks him under the water, then picks up a soft bristle brush and scrubs his whole body. She steps out of the pool and motions for him to sit on the edge, then stands behind him, untangling his hair with her fingers. Enkidu feels her hands like two small animals, both of them doing their small animal things. The stubborn knots of hair she cuts off with a small bronze razor. The places where Enkidu has scrapes or insect bites she cuts close to the skin.

With a touch, she lifts his upper arm and he stands up from the side of the warm pool. She leads him into the fresh pool to rinse. Then she dries him with a coarse linen cloth.

Afterwards, she goes over his hair and beard and body with a wide ivory comb, trimming here and there to even out the patchwork she's made. He's not going to look fashionable and she guesses that he doesn't care.

When Shamhat brings out the scented oil, Enkidu pulls away. She will use the plain oil instead. She rubs his scalp and his feet and his hands. She has the boy fetch a wool skirt, but when offered to Enkidu he ignores it.

Then Shamhat takes Enkidu's hand, and leads him out of the baths, down one corridor and then another, where they meet a large eunuch posted at a doorway. Shamhat nods to the eunuch. The eunuch bows and opens the door for them, and they walk through to the courtyard and Enkidu's new room.

The boy had filled the water pitcher and left a tray on the sleeping platform. There are flat breads, a cup of cow milk, and a warm bowl of braised lamb chunks in a thin spicy sauce.

Shamhat faces Enkidu, still holding his hand. She sees the small changes in his face, outward ripples of some deeper movement.

Pressing her free hand to her chest, she says, "Shamhat."

Enkidu nods, says "Sham-hat," then pauses. Among his people he has many names, some of them are secret.

Who is this woman, Shamhat, and how much should he reveal to her? He puts his hand to his chest and says, "Enkidu."

She repeats, "En-ki-du."

She picks up a flat bread from the tray, says her word "food" and Enkidu repeats it. The pitcher of water, "water." She leads him out to the courtyard and points to a sloping channel cut into the stone floor, a handbreadth from the south wall.

It looks clean to the eye, but Enkidu can smell it. So that's what these people do since they've covered up the soil. Shamhat nods, she can see that he understands the channel's purpose. She gets a clay jar from the corner, dips it in the pool, and shows Enkidu how to rinse the latrine. The water drains through an opening cut into the wall.

Shamhat smiles. Enkidu is learning quickly.

She moves her hands, miming something about how she is leaving now, but will return later. If he wants anything just call out, and the boy will try to understand him and bring it. She kisses his face again, goes back through the door, and the eunuch closes it behind her.

— 2 —

Enkidu paces the courtyard. He feels his feet pressing cut stone instead of living soil. A scattering of ants patrol the crevices in the paving. They haven't found anything worth massing a line.

He sits on the stone floor, his back against a wall. He looks at the square of sky up above. Beyond the walls, he doesn't see any trees or buildings, only sky. Sounds come to him from unknown distances and directions. There are voices and human activity, musical instruments, the bleat of sheep.

Enkidu watches the shadow of the wall slowly move across the courtyard. The line where light meets dark traces the cracks and texture of the stone floor. A beetle is walking across the paving, crossing from sun to shadow. It then raises its wings and flies in a circle back to the sunlight. The sky changes colors with the hours and the weather. A sparrow flutters in, hops and cocks its head, finds a crumb, picks it up, and bustles back over the wall.

Sometimes, there are clouds, but the sky is almost never fully clear. Often yellow in the mornings, pale pink-orange in the evenings. The blue of midday is hazed with smoke and thin clouds.

One morning the courtyard was wet from an overnight rain. The sky was a perfect blue until the sun had nearly reached its highest point.

Enkidu floats in the pool.

One evening he heard a gaggle of crows flying over. He saw a dark flash of wingtip wave into his square of sky.

The boy brings meals three times a day.

Enkidu has learned the words for a variety of foods.

This is not a way for a man to live. He could leave here. Fight his way out, go somewhere else. He is aware of the possibility, but he hasn't felt that urge, not yet.

And where is Ninsigal? Can he feel her nearby? There is so much noise in the city that everything gets mixed up. Though he has the feeling that leaving here would only take him farther from her.

What if he went looking for her in the city? Where would he look? Who would help him? Passing through the city on the way to the temple, no one greeted him. He mostly noticed fear, if they reacted to him at all.

There is nothing to do but wait. When he is out on the land hunting, most of what he does is wait. This is not the same as that.

Every evening Shamhat comes to visit Enkidu. She brings food and they talk. Enkidu's days are uneventful, yet somehow there is plenty to talk about. In the first few days, he learned the words "barley cake" and "cucumber" and "beer."

He has discovered that he is interested in learning her language.

He also found that he is good at it. Shamhat can say a few things in his language. She knows "greetings cousin" and "may you have good health." He calls her Shamhat. She calls him Enkidu.

The city language is different from the way Enkidu's people speak. It is patterns of sounds put together to signify things. A collection of sounds made with the mouth. Some of the sounds they put next to each other are so strange that Enkidu can't help but laugh.

He has not seen any sign that the city people feel their language in their bodies. He might ask Shamhat about this when he learns enough words. At this point, he feels like his little nephew, not able to speak more than a short string, and only in a single line. But this language seems to require nothing more than memory to master. That he can do.

He watches her lips and her eyes. She speaks with more than just her voice. Her expressions color the words. Her eyes widen when he understands a difficult phrase. When they get to body parts, Enkidu smiles. He makes her show him again.

They begin telling each other stories in the city language, using their hands to help explain. Enkidu can usually guess the meanings of new words. He asks her to repeat them so he can be sure. He tells her about Ninsigal and how they were going to be married. She nods and holds his hand to her heart.

At the end of their visits, Shamhat and Enkidu have sex. In the beginning, he felt awkward. He hadn't had much experience as a man with a woman, and he didn't know the customs of these city people. But Shamhat put him at ease.

She comes toward him with confidence, and he follows her eyes as she moves to meet him. She takes his hands and brings him to-ward her. A nod or small hand movement to show him what she likes. She has no trouble reading the signs of his body.

It doesn't seem to be a problem, what he knows or doesn't know. He marvels: she is so skilled at giving and taking pleasure. It's much like the way he knows bird calls and animal traces, except she is just one other person in a small plastered room.

Enkidu speaks to the boy. He has now learned words for much more than just food. The boy has brought the morning meal, and Enkidu stops him before he leaves the courtyard.

"She said I can ask you to bring what I need. I came here to look for my friend Ninsigal. Can you find her for me?"

The boy nods, "I can try. How will I know her?"

Enkidu describes her.

"She is like me, from the land, not the city. About the same height as Shamhat. A grown woman, but younger, unmarried. Or not married when I last saw her. Her hair is black like mine, long but not quite so curly. She ties her hair with braided grass bands. She wore a broad weave linen dress with seed beads woven into the hem."

Enkidu continues. "Her shoulders are wider than her hips, strong bones, working hands and feet. She has a visible scar just above her left ankle bone on the outside of the leg. She was stolen from her family by bandits, about the new moon before the summer solstice. The place they captured her was a nine-day walk west of here."

The boy nods again and says, "I'll see what I can find out."

The boy goes out on his daily errands. He meets servants from rich houses as they do their rounds, he talks with the gossips at the city gates and porters arriving with caravans from other cities. He gives them his smile and he watches their faces as they speak, and people enjoy telling him their tales.

He hears a variety of stories, though none sound quite like Enkidu's friend. But there are so many stories, surely there are more yet to hear. Everyone knows that the city has rich and pow-erful men who keep young women as slaves. And certain of those slaves are never seen by anyone, not even the house servants. Perhaps Ninsigal has been made one of those, but it would be difficult to find out.

He will keep his eyes open.

Enkidu listens with interest as the boy tells of people coming and going in the city. About servants, and aristocrats, and caravan traders. He is learning about the way people in the city make their livings. About what you can know by the clothing that they wear.

The boy has brought a board, and they start playing the pebble game when he visits. Enkidu learns numbers and counting from the boy. He already knew about how quick little fingers can make a play to cheat. The boy laughs when Enkidu catches him, then tries another method. Enkidu has started calling him "little brother."

One evening Enkidu tries to tell Shamhat the story of the rabbit and the fox. Since there is no word in the city language for the sense of knowing that comes up from the ground, he has to simplify his telling. This makes the story a different kind of funny. Shamhat knows a tale of a rabbit and a fox, so she fills in some of the words, trying to help. But the stories don't quite match up. Before they have finished they break down laughing, the rabbit and fox are left facing each other, confused. The story has turned into a long circling joke about long ears catching fuzzy meanings, telling furry tales.

Later, Enkidu asks Shamhat a question. "You're always gone a long time. What do you do all day?"

She laughs, loosens her hair, and leans back against the wall. Enkidu sees her watching his face, a little smile, her eyes soften. She shifts to ease her wrap around her belly and takes a deep breath. She will answer his question, but she will need to explain many things, and they won't finish in only one evening.

Shamhat's life is interwoven with the life of the city, and explaining a whole city will take some time. She starts by saying that she serves as a Lady of the Temple to Inanna.

"We here at the temple of Inanna take pleasure in our service to the goddess. And to please her, many of us have come together to give life to her home. This room where you live, and the little courtyard and the baths, and the room you first arrived in are but a small part of the whole temple, set a little apart from much of the daily practice we perform."

"There are many other rooms in the temple," she says, "and many other people who make their lives here. Some people only carry out their days with their work here, while they live elsewhere in the city. There are many different tasks that people perform at the temple, and several ranks of officials here at the temple make sure that the work goes as it should."

Enkidu sits next to her, his thigh touching hers as he listens. Her body heat is steady, while her words ebb and flow. While she speaks he leans a bit forward. He sees their feet on the floor while he hears her voice. His feet are wide and hairy compared to hers. His toes are thick. Hers are finer and smooth, a warm color in the reflected sunset.

He gets up to pour her a cup of water. She nods her thanks and drinks deeply. When she puts the cup down beside her, Enkidu takes her hand and brings her to stand with him. Her palm is warm. He leads her out to the courtyard and they walk a lazy circle around the pool. Enkidu holds her hand and tilts his head to her voice, his eyes move between her face and the fading colors of the sky above the wall.

Shamhat looks straight ahead as she speaks. She says that her main purpose at the temple is ministering to the women here.

He asks her, "Who are the women? What do they do here?"

She tells him, "Some arrive here as very young girls, they are orphans, or sometimes they are brought by someone who then goes away without a word. Others are widows, or widows in name. They come because they've lost their husbands, or because they must escape their husbands, or because they don't have husbands but their families say they must. Some come as young women, often still just girls, fleeing a marriage their family is forcing on them.

"The temple gives them a place to live and fitting tasks for their days. It is my duty to see that all the women of Inanna get the shelter and useful work that they require, for as long as they choose to stay here. Our temple performs many services that maintain the city, just like the temple of Anu. You doubtless saw Anu on the next hill when you first came here."

Enkidu slips his hand from Shamhat's and reaches around her waist, palm on her ribs and fingers at the soft place below. He matches his steps to hers as they walk, holding her hip to his thigh. She puts her near hand at the small of his back, he can feel the heat of her inner arm on his ribs.

Shamhat continues, "One of our main devotions here at the temple is making the daily meals for Inanna, the goddess, and this requires many people, both women and men. We slaughter and dress the livestock and game birds, cook the meat and boil the broth, grind flour and bake the bread, and malt the grain and brew beer. There are also the singers whose vocation is chanting to the goddess while the food is being prepared."

"We have women who set the table for the goddess," she says, "and then afterward present the meal of Inanna to everyone here within the temple, and to those outside the temple who come to share Inanna's blessing. These are the meals that we also share with you.

"We also please the goddess by spinning and weaving. Many women spend their days here making wool and linen fabric to clothe the people of Uruk, also to send on the caravans to trade with other cities."

The sunset has fallen to deep reds and greys, and the air become still and humid. Shamhat's effort at explaining has raised a sweat along her hairline. She takes her hand from Enkidu's back and loosens his arm around her, shrugging her wrap from her back and shoulders. She takes a loop of cloth and skims it over her face and neck and between her breasts, then wraps the length of fabric around her waist, tucking it in. Enkidu watches the movement of her chest and hands. He smiles and puts his arm back around her, his hand higher on her ribs.

Shamhat goes on with her list, "We also maintain stockyards for the herds of animals which feed the goddess, and granaries to store the harvest from season to season. We have teams of scribes who keep records of all the materials that come to the temple, all the finished items that we produce, and the items that we gain from trading. The temple scribes also record other transactions for the people of the city who come to us for that service. And our priests use these records as needed when they sit in judgment of disputes."

"And," she adds, "we have our temple scholars who devote themselves to watching the sky, and they mark the days of the celebrations throughout the year."

Enkidu slips his hand from Shamhat's ribs to the curve above her thigh. He watches her face, chest, and belly. There is no visible detail in the fading dusk light, only shape and movement.

Shamhat keeps on, "The annual festivals bring the largest numbers of people to the temple, when we celebrate the days of Inanna, along with the other gods of the seasons. These celebrations are the heart of the city, what holds us together as citizens of Uruk."

"I'm sure that you'd recognize some of the rites, we have been doing them for many generations, and they have not changed so very much since the time when our ancestors first settled in this place and built the city to live in. Our historians tell us that it was these celebrations that brought people together in their seasons, and then the people wanted to maintain the spirit of the festival and keep living together throughout the year. Thus, over time, they grew to become the city as we have it."

She turns her face toward him. "Though perhaps it is the daily coupling rituals that are most particular to Inanna. It is one of my duties to see that these also run properly. Certain of our women perform the rites of Inanna's sex with the men of the city."

Enkidu pulls back his arm and turns to look Shamhat in the eyes. His eyes are wide open, and he shakes his head.

He says, "I understand men wanting sex. But for a woman to have it her duty to give it to them? What kind of job is that? Don't the men have families? Don't they have friends? Don't they know their neighbors? Do the men even know the names of the temple women? What has happened to these men's families that they need a temple to provide a family for them?"

Shamhat reaches out to take Enkidu's hand which he is still holding out in front of him. She is aware that her culture is very different from his. She understands that he might be outraged. She is merely telling him her people's customs, whatever their reasons.

Why it should be so, and how it could be different? Those are big questions, the answers doubtless not what we expect.

She holds his hand with both of hers. "I know that your people live differently than we do here in the city, and I know these differences run through our whole society. We are settled, and you keep moving. We have many possessions, and you keep only the things that you are willing to carry. But mothers in Uruk still love their children, and fathers still work to provide for their families."

She says, "But when there are so many of us in the city living so closely together, it's not that simple anymore. We have to make new rules and find new ways for people to get what they need. It can be surprising what people might require to stay together as a city."

Enkidu loosens and lowers their hands. Shamhat keeps her eyes on his, pausing a moment before she takes back the hand that she had been using for gestures.

"But I should explain a little more about the sex ritual and the women who do it. This practice began long ago when the city was yet new. At the start of the year, we would please the goddess with our bodies, seeking her favor for our freshly planted fields. Many of us believe that the goddess takes pleasure from sex in the temple, and she responds by giving us her blessings in turn. Other people see it as a practical way to soothe the passions of men in the city who might otherwise cause trouble. But in any case, sex is only given by the women who choose this role, and the young ones are not free to choose this before they have reached womanhood."

Shamhat takes a step forward, leading Enkidu to resume walking with her. "When a man comes to Inanna, he may state his preferences, but the choices belong to the women. First the priestess at the temple door, then the woman in the appointed chamber. That woman tells the man what she requires, and the man must do it or he must leave the temple. If she requires him to bathe, he must bathe. If the gift he brings is not generous, she may reject it. If he threatens her, the eunuchs throw him out.

"Her task is to please the goddess by giving the man release, but the woman chooses the method. If the man harms her, she chooses how the eunuchs punish him. They can make a new eunuch faster than you can clean a fish. The temple women can choose that too, and everyone knows this."

Shamhat waits a breath, then says, "Certain women are suited to such a life. Inside the temple walls, they are able to enjoy men without being ruled by them, they can be the body of the goddess without all the complications that come with life outside the temple.

Shamhat turns to meet Enkidu's eyes, "When I was younger, I performed these rites too. Now I have many other duties, and I am more selective. Now the eunuchs allow no one into my chamber unless I give the word."

Enkidu bends his elbow to look at her hand in his. His fingers are blunt with hair between the knuckles. Her fingers are long for a woman, but still shorter than his. He stops walking, turns toward her, and lets out a breath. She brings his hand to her lips and then leads him back to his room.

Their sex takes longer this time.

Before Enkidu kisses her, he pulls up her wrap to cover her breasts, even though the light has fully fallen and there is no sight, only touch. He pauses with his hand on her cheek. She has the same face she had yesterday, even when she closes her eyes.

She raises her face to his, lifts a hand, and puts it on his cheek, fingertips find the coarse hair of his beard. Then she gets up and unwinds her wrap, stepping out of the fabric. She settles back down beside him in the dark.

— 4 —

Enkidu has many thoughts filling his long days. This language of the city is well made for putting words onto things. It is useful for explaining. But before he learned these words, he doesn't remember having need for them. What this new language calls thoughts or ideas, he would simply feel without putting a name on them. And his family always seemed to understand him.

Or, he might not even have a feeling of an idea, just simply take action, and in the doing see that it was the right thing. These new words have great power. They can describe what he sees and feels. They can also make things more confusing. It is possible to know certain things in words, and this makes them seem more solid. But there are more things to know than words to put on them.

Enkidu stands at the door to the corridor and shouts, "Hey eunuch, come in here and wrestle!"

The eunuch opens the door and stands blocking the way. The eunuch is almost as big as Enkidu and shows no fear.

The eunuch calls the boy and sends him to ask the Lady.

Enkidu and the eunuch stand facing each other. Arms crossed and feet set wide, staring each other down. The boy returns, saying that the eunuch may wrestle Enkidu. Not to worry about Enkidu escaping, he could always leave freely if he wanted to.

When Enkidu hears this he is more confused than before. The eunuch rushes forward and flips him to the floor.

They were almost evenly matched. Not long ago, Enkidu would have beaten this eunuch easily, but he has gotten soft, and this eunuch is very skilled. Wrestling a eunuch is not the same as wrestling his cousins. The eunuchs shave off all their hair and oil their bodies, making it hard to get a grip. Where most men have aggression that pushes them forward, the eunuch has strategy, using only the force necessary to accomplish the move.

Enkidu is happy. This kind of wrestling is really fun. He smiles at describing it to himself with words. The eunuch shows no feeling, but that doesn't matter. They will do this again tomorrow.

⚖◇

When Shamhat comes that evening, they do their greetings without words. She puts her hands behind his neck and looks up to his eyes. She bends him down and kisses his mouth.

He pulls her close to him. Picks her up and carries her to the sleeping platform. This is when he notices she is naked — not even the thin fabric of her wrap between them.

Later, she calls the boy since she hadn't brought a tray. "Bring double this time, Enkidu is finally hungry."

They eat quietly, admiring each other in the fading light from the courtyard. He sees her affection in the lifting of her cheeks. He hadn't been certain before.

They arrive at the time when their routine is to have sex. They start again, but there is no hurry, only the soft pressure of her body and the texture of her hair.

She has found a knot in his back muscle, and she's reaching around to massage it. He puts a fingertip to the midpoint of her brow, the arc of her jaw, and the curve of her chin.

This is nice, but they miss their conversation. Using their voices, not just eyes and hands. What do lovers say at times like this?

It is not the words that matter, it is the tone and the hearing.

The talk is for soothing. But soon the words will either fade away or become more solid and gain meaning.

— 5 —

Then one evening, Shamhat doesn't come.

Enkidu is aware that he has been relying on her. That hadn't been a problem until now. What is he really doing here anyway?

His confusion begins souring to annoyance. Then, the courtyard door opens. An old woman comes in and sets a tray of food on the floor. Enkidu notices the woman's hands: they are large, the skin worn red from years of labor. She doesn't look at him and retreats behind the door before he can question her.

Enkidu's stomach rumbles without hunger.

He squats and picks at the food on the tray. Where is Shamhat? Where is the boy? What if he just walks out of the temple? Why does he even stay here in Uruk?

Did he really believe that a temple woman would love him? And what about Ninsigal?

He could leave the city. But why did he come here in the first place?

Enkidu gets to his feet and paces around the edges of the courtyard. He marches to the wall, turns to the left, and keeps going until this marching makes no sense.

He sits down beside the pool and then leans back. He rests his head on the floor and stares at the hazy night sky. In the morning, he gets up and paces the courtyard in the opposite direction.

The old woman brings more food. Enkidu looks at the tray by the door. The morning meal. His feet on the lingering night coolness of the stone floor.

He pushes through the door. Out past the eunuch and down the corridor. He hasn't seen this place since the day he first arrived and his memory is unclear. He decides his direction by the sound of voices coming from a room up ahead.

Turning a corner, he arrives in a room with two long tables where a dozen women are preparing large quantities of food. Those at one table chop piles of onions and roots, those at the other slice strips of meat from the butchered haunches of sheep.

At the head of the room is an old woman in a long linen robe. She is singing a song of praise to Inanna. The working women hum along with her or chat quietly among themselves as they chop and slice. When the women see Enkidu enter, everything stops. They all stare at him.

The woman in the long robe comes to Enkidu and tells him that he shouldn't be here, pointing the way back out of the room. The other women keep staring at him. Enkidu nods to the old woman and goes back the way he came.

What was he expecting to find, wandering around the temple?

He walks back down the corridor to his courtyard, past the eunuch at the doorway, who watches him without expression.

He sits down with his back against the courtyard wall, face in full sun. Heat on his forehead and red glow behind closed eyelids.

What a strange place these city people have made.

⚶⊕◇

In the evening the door opens, and Shamhat walks through. She comes to Enkidu with a hand held toward him.

He catches her wrist. "Where were you?"

Her eyes look tired. "There are a lot of things happening at the temple right now."

Enkidu says, "Tell me."

Shamhat looks at Enkidu's hand where he has caught her. "Listen, I've been arguing with people for two whole days, and I was hoping to come here and get some rest."

Enkidu feels the heat of anger rising up his sternum. Anger expands upward in his throat, but catches at the back of his tongue and gets no further. As the rising subsides, he releases her wrist, and she rubs it with her other hand. She looks up, and he meets her eyes but he can't read them, though she doesn't move away.

The moment stretches, and the distance between them isn't decreasing. How much can you really know of another person?

Then he remembers his friend Shamhat. Enkidu takes a half step forward and puts his arms around her. She keeps her shape, and he holds her lightly, awkward. But they are touching, and their breathing starts to adjust.

Her body loosens a little and he can shape himself to her.

They have been lovers for long enough that they have met in many different moods, but their meeting has never required much effort. Closing the distance between them this time will not be so simple.

As he waits for her, a thought occurs to him. Until now he hasn't needed to draw her toward him. She has always come by her own choice. But he is not creeping up on a bird that will fly at the smallest sound. She is much more solid than that. There is something heavy in her that he likely can't lift.

He stands still and calms his breathing. He gives her his attention, but lightly. He can feel the reserve in the eye of her heart.

It won't open until it is ready.

He can feel the change as she remembers her friend Enkidu.

She says, "Just let me sleep here tonight."

— 6 —

They awake in the morning, cloudy dawn light turning from orange to yellow-grey. The boy brings a tray with melons and cheese. They sit beside each other on the platform, backs to the wall, arms touching, and the tray at Enkidu's thigh.

In the morning light, things look different than they did in last night's dusk. Enkidu is still not sure what Shamhat is thinking. He can feel the distance where his arm touches hers, though it is less sharp than it was the night before.

There is a warm place inside his sternum. Another warm place between his legs, it was strange to sleep with her without sex.

He watches the small moves her body makes as she breathes. Enkidu looks up and sees Shamhat watching his face. How long has she been looking at him and he didn't notice?

She wants to speak, maybe that will help.

Enkidu's eyes say that he's listening.

Shamhat begins, "I have lived at the temple of Inanna since I was a girl. I remember some things from the time before that, but I only have a few pieces, and they don't come together to make a story. And certainly, by now, I feel like my whole life is here. The temple is all of my family and my closest friends.

"But it is also a large institution serving the city. And when many people come together as a group, as we do when we make the temple, all those people working toward the same goal cause a lot of power to come together all in one place. With this power, it is possible to do great work, but it can also happen that the power gets abused.

"You could say that Inanna is like one of your nomad clans, except larger, and our tents are made of brick instead of sheep's wool. And the city of Uruk is like one of your seasonal meetings, but always here in our place by the river. Of course, this is not exact, but maybe a picture like this can help explain how we do things in the city. The other temples and the rich families are each like some of your clans too."

Enkidu notices that her voice is different when she talks about the politics of the temple and the city. She speaks a little louder and the words make sharper edges. Her forehead tenses, and she speaks to a point in front of her, just out of reach.

She asks him, "Do you remember when you told me about how your people meet up during the season of the goose migration? How all the clans must agree on how many geese to take and what portion goes to each family? Well, here at the temples we do something similar, we apportion the grain harvest and the other crops that the farmers produce, the sheep and the cattle from the herdsmen, the things that the artisans make, and the goods that the traders bring from far away."

"You have seen how many people there are in the city. All of them want something for themselves and for their families. The bargaining is fierce and there are many disagreements, but among the leaders of the temples we can usually find a way for everyone to get what they need."

Shamhat pauses and lets out a breath. Enkidu sees a thought pass across her forehead before she continues. He looks down at his hands as they rest in his lap, interweaving his fingers.

She goes on, "Yes, it is true that the temples keep a lot of wealth for ourselves, and the rich families get much more than their true portion. There are reasons why this happens, and I won't speak of them now. But up until recently, we thought our methods were working, that we could live well as many people in one city. By collecting all our labor together, many minds and many muscles, the results add up to much more than if each person acted alone. You have seen some of the great works that the city makes possible."

She pauses, watching the side of his face until he looks up from the hands in his lap and meets her eyes.

She lays a hand on his and continues, "I know our people do things differently from yours, and you may not choose to live the way we do, but I love the life of the city. And I have believed that we could still share the wealth of the city fairly with everyone here, even as we grew greater and gained more. Fairly enough, anyway.

She takes a breath, lifting her shoulders, "Now I fear that I was wrong. There is the tyrant, Gilgamesh. He is like a whole other clan by himself. If you haven't heard his name, you have seen his soldiers. He has broken the old bargains. He simply takes whatever he wants with no thought for anyone else."

"We have seen selfish people before, but never with so much power. The tyrant buys his soldier's loyalty, and nothing withstands their compounded greed, not to mention their weapons.

She says, "We are not surprised by greed, over the years we have come to expect it. But we always thought that the powerful men would remember the agreements at the foundation of the city. That they must not take too much and push the people into poverty. These are the things that the priests and officials are arguing about. Up until now, we thought that by working together, Inanna and Anu temples could keep Gilgamesh under control, or at least limit his ability to pay his army."

Enkidu has gone back to examining his hands. Shamhat has taken back her hand so she can go on talking.

"But Inanna and Anu are no longer of the same mind. Gilgamesh's mother Ninsun is working to overthrow Lilitu, our high priestess here at Inanna. This has caused disruption among the priests and the nobles, and they have started drawing up sides and fighting for their own power. If the Ninsun faction wins, she will have the temple of Inanna support the tyrant. And there are other ambitious people besides Lilitu and Ninsun, they have their own schemes and plans for how to run the temple. But among all the various factions it seems that everyone is much more interested in gaining power than doing the work of the temple."

Enkidu nods and leans his head back against the wall. He looks at the bright patch of the courtyard outside his doorway.

Shamhat says, "I have been arguing with the priests, I keep trying to find the words to say how I feel about the temple. It's my home. I argue with them like they are my family — I feel like they are my family, but no matter what I say, I don't get the feeling that they consider me to be part of their family in return. They seem unable to look beyond the competition for power. I don't know what else to do. I'm sure I'll keep on talking, but I don't hear anyone listening to me."

She stops for a moment, letting her hands drop to her sides, "Ay! That was a long story. Hand me a slice of melon."

Enkidu still says nothing. He hands her a slice of melon and takes some for himself. Shamhat's face has come to rest with her lips in a straight line.

She takes a breath before she begins eating her melon slice, then tilts her head back against the wall when she has finished. The heat of the morning is rising, so she loosens her wrap. She reaches for his hand before she continues.

"When you first arrived here, I was mostly just curious, who is this large naked man? Now I see more of you, I see that you are more than just a large naked man, that your strength is not only in your muscles and bones. You have a sense for other people, it often feels like you understand what I mean, even more than the words that I say. And you seem to have a sense for your strength, you don't use it to take advantage, you have a way of getting what you want without needing to use force."

Then, meeting his eyes, she adds, "Which is why I was so surprised by how you acted last night."

Enkidu looks back to his lap. He turns to pick up another slice of melon and hand it to her. All this talk is heating the back of his head. Now that Shamhat has started talking about him, the heat is spreading to his temples. She still hasn't told him what part he plays in her story.

Shamhat takes the melon slice, but before she takes a bite, she goes on talking, "I was telling you about the conflict here at the temple, how the people struggling for power seem to have lost their feeling for working together if they ever had it. But there's more than that. Gilgamesh has heard of your arrival in Uruk. He is vain and superstitious and has the idea that you were brought here especially for him, as a sign from the gods. Gilgamesh's mother wants him to take you as his ally and then go and conquer the other kings along the river."

She continues, "Lilitu and the priests of Anu believe that since you are here with me at Inanna, you will take their side and fight against Ninsun. They believe that if you challenge Gilgamesh, it might bring him back to good sense, or at least distract him from driving Uruk to ruin. It's possible that could work."

She lifts her chin, "But in any case, it seems that Gilgamesh is fascinated by what he has heard about you. He and his chief soldiers are now in Kish arguing with the king there, and soon he will be returning. I know that you have no interest in the little squabbles of our city. I know that you and your people see things much differently than we do. For a long time that didn't matter much because there was so little contact between our peoples. It seemed that you were able to keep your distance."

She finally bites the melon slice, taking a moment, "But the distance is shrinking. Surely you have noticed that the tyrant has an effect far out into the hinterlands. We hear stories about bandits raiding the countryside and kidnapping your people. Many of those stories speak of the bandits wearing the red skirt of Gilgamesh's army."

The end of
the middle of
the middle.

THREE

— I —

Later that morning Enkidu called the eunuch and they wrestled again, setting aside all the words and all the meanings of the day and the night before.

The exertion of wrestling moves blood to muscle. Blood moves the heat at his temples from when Shamhat was speaking and moves the tightness behind his ribs that he woke up with.

Muscles make their own heat, mix and pass to lungs and breathe out, like wind blowing mist off the surface of water.

They grip and tumble. They grunt as bodies hit the floor. Enkidu's sweat mixes with oil from the eunuch's skin. Two animal bodies pulling and twisting, joined together by their efforts. The eunuch is learning there is more than just winning and losing.

Afterward, Enkidu's mind feels warm, both empty and filled, with the taste of good hunger at the back of his palate, his skin just the right shape to fit his body.

The boy brought a meal of roasted goat and onions.

It wasn't his strength he'd been missing so much as his spirit. He bathed, then slept through the height of the sun, and when he woke he asked the eunuch to bring another and they three would wrestle together.

That evening when Shamhat comes to meet him, he tells her that he wants to go outside to see the city. They walk from Enkidu's courtyard to her rooms where she straps on leather sandals and drapes a thin linen shawl to cover her arms. They walk together through the temple colonnade to the plaza. Enkidu marvels again at the patterns of colored tiles along the front of the temple.

The light is falling and the public crowd has thinned. People are going back to their shelters for the night. Shamhat and Enkidu walk side by side around the plaza. A few people see them walking and stare at the Lady out in public with a big naked man. Someone remembers seeing Enkidu when he first arrived in the city. They point at the Lady and tell the story among their friends.

Back in Enkidu's room, he is still hungry. He calls the boy to bring more meat, but not any beer. Shamhat leans back, done with her dinner. Their previous conversation remains unfinished. She sits quietly, her hands folded and eyes on his face.

Enkidu knows she is waiting for him to respond. Would he ally with them against Gilgamesh? Enkidu has no way to answer this, so he considers the other parts of the story.

Shamhat has spoken less than usual that evening. She is thoughtful, noticing the air changing between them. Enkidu goes out to the courtyard pool and washes the dinner scraps from his beard. He looks up. The stars are hidden by haze. The moon is old and hasn't risen yet. The words of the last few days still hum in his ears.

He walks back to the room and sits down beside Shamhat. Picking up her left hand he examines its back side, the shadow of veins crossing tendons in the space between wrist and knuckles. He knows this hand, at least certain sides of it.

She is waiting for him to say something, but what he knows is hard to tell in words.

He begins speaking slowly. "I came here because of Ninsigal, and I haven't forgotten her. But that was before. Now, after many days and nights here, things are different.

"You remember how it was when I first arrived. How you came to me. How my eyes were filled with this beautiful woman. I was caught up in your attentions. Now, I see how you have begun to love me. And how I love you too. But I can not see how you would be my wife. Would you be my wife?"

He waits for a moment. A smile crosses his face, then fades, "No, I didn't think so. But this is what I expected. It doesn't change how I feel for you. I have learned some of your language. Now I can speak these thoughts to you, but still, the stories we tell are so different. Yes, our bodies tell the same story, and that pleases me very much. But I don't share your concerns for the temple and the city, even if I might understand them a little. These last few days I have been remembering my family and my homeland. I would go to them now, but whatever brought me here isn't done yet. I feel it, and for now, I don't know more than that."

Enkidu stands up and crosses to the doorway, then turns and comes back to stand in front of Shamhat. "This conflict that you have been telling me about — surely there is more to it than I understand. But I believe you when you say that you wish to serve the temple and the city. So yes, if it is what you want, I will agree to meet this king Gilgamesh and take his measure. I can't promise more than that. Even though our aims are different, they might take the same path, at least for now. We'll see what comes next."

— 2 —

Gilgamesh has come back to Uruk and the movement of the city has quickened. Rich men and their attendants press together at the palace entrance. At the back of the palace, donkeys shift their feet, burdened with baskets filled with food. More soldiers strut through the crowds on the streets. The king's people weave through the markets looking for goods to satisfy the desires of the palace.

At the market stalls, women take less time gossiping with their friends and they hurry back to their houses. Farmers spend longer days in the fields, they don't come back inside for the mid-day rest, or linger at the gates trading news. Nobles stationed at the gates look more closely at the parcels people carry. Priests meet at the temples, leaning in, and speak quietly with each other in serious tones.

Enkidu and Shamhat are walking in the temple plaza again when she tells Enkidu that the tyrant and his men have returned from Kish, and they're back at the palace. He nods, thoughtful, then asks, "What do you know about the men who kidnap my people?"

She answers, "As I told you, I've heard that some of those bandits are the king's soldiers, but we don't see them here at the temple, so I don't know much more than that. The kidnappers don't bring stolen women to us because we won't pay them, and soldiers don't enter the temple because the eunuchs will take their weapons. Thus, I know only what I have been told. The stories I hear say that the bandits sell the young women as slaves, either to rich men here in Uruk or to passing trade caravans. Others of the women are kept in the tyrant's palace harem to service him and his guests. Our temple works closely with some of the powerful men in the city, but those men don't tell us what they do privately in their houses."

She unlaces her arm from Enkidu's so she can use both hands for gestures. "There are other rich men who are more tightly allied with Gilgamesh, and most of what we know of their dealings comes to us indirectly. Though sometimes when they grow tired of their slaves they bring them to us at the temple. In those cases, we provide the woman a home if she wishes to stay. I have heard rumors that one or two of Gilgamesh's ministers may have gotten a new slave woman lately, but I couldn't say whether one of them is Ninsigal."

"And what about the king?" he asks her. "Our people don't have kings, but your people do. How do you decide whether you have a good king or not? You have told me a little about Gilgamesh. But how is he more of a problem than any other king you might have?"

Shamhat gives him a sad chuckle and shrugs. "Yes, I know what you mean. Kings can be many kinds of problems, and Gilgamesh is really not much different than the other kings, except that he gives us so many more of the usual kinds of problems. He knows no restraint, and he doesn't listen when his people cry for relief. His soldiers force men into work gangs, and he claims all the virgins in the city before they sleep with their new husbands."

Enkidu's eyes go wide and he stops and turns to stare at her when she says this. Color rises to his face. Stealing men's wives! Just like they stole Ninsigal! He feels his heart speed up, a tension in his hands. Shamhat reaches to take his hand and waits for his breath to settle.

Shamhat and Enkidu have gone out walking two other times since that first evening, and he is beginning to get a feel for how people move in the city. The city people don't walk like Enkidu's people out in the wild lands, each on their own line. Instead, they seem more like herd animals. They move as a group, a little skittish.

Watching people, he looks to the distance to see people who haven't noticed him. The people nearby always stop what they were doing and stare at him. They don't give him any useful clues. This only increases his longing for his family, who give him no extra attention.

As they walk, Enkidu asks Shamhat to show him the houses of the rich men, the ones she has heard rumors about. So they go to the rich neighborhoods, and she tells him what she knows of the people who live in each of the houses they pass.

Enkidu marvels at the rich people he sees. They have so many possessions, all of them finely made. The rich people are so different from the farmers and laborers. They hold themselves erect, faces tilted upward. As if they have no worry for their wants being satisfied, or what labor that satisfaction might require.

This evening they are out walking a little earlier, the sun is just setting and people are hurrying to finish their errands. They pass a large house whose entry is filled with people wearing finely made clothing. Musicians spill onto the street. Everyone is laughing and drinking. The whole crowd is dressed in fine clothing and none of the usual laborers can be seen. For once, all these people don't notice Enkidu.

They are singing a song to someone inside the house. Shamhat explains that this is a wedding party, the bride's family has just brought her to the young man's father's house, and the marriage ceremony is almost completed.

Up the street, coming toward them, a flash of bronze and brightly colored fabric. Soldiers, big men marching quickly, wearing bright red sheepskin skirts.

Shamhat turns to Enkidu, "If you are ready to meet Gilgamesh, you only need to keep standing right here."

Enkidu nods and widens his stance. Shamhat keeps her hand held in his.

Twelve soldiers, maybe fifteen, approach on a quick march. At their center marches a man nearly a head taller. He is young, with oiled black hair and a short beard, wearing a wide leather belt and long sheepskin skirt dyed deep purple. The marching soldiers don't look to the side. They stomp right past and crash into the house with the party.

Everyone starts yelling, and the guests scramble out of the house and run in every direction. The noise gets louder and Gilgamesh strides back out the door. Two soldiers follow him, carrying a young woman like a log on their shoulders. Flowers shake loose from her hair as she struggles against the soldier's grip. There is a tear in her fine linen tunic.

Enkidu takes a run and dives at Gilgamesh's knees. He slams Gilgamesh's head on the street and cracks an elbow across his cheekbone.

Gilgamesh tries to twist away and grabs for Enkidu's eyes. One of the soldiers moves to join the fight.

Enkidu kicks the soldier's feet out from under him. Three women from the crowd throw an urn of beer. It hits the soldiers carrying the bride.

The soldiers drop the girl and chase after the women. The bridegroom and father-in-law jump out of the crowd, pick up the bride, and rush her around the side of the house.

Enkidu and Gilgamesh are a grunting mass of limbs rolling in the street. Shamhat has found someone she knows in the crowd and sends her running to fetch the temple eunuchs. The soldiers keep trying to hit Enkidu, but the fight rolls around too fast. The women are yelling and kicking at the soldiers, and the boys are pelting them with lumps of food.

This time the virgin bride has escaped un-raped. But Enkidu doesn't notice, he is too busy trying to pry Gilgamesh's fist from his beard or free his leg to deliver another knee to his groin. Gilgamesh is energized, swinging wildly. He is not very skilled, but his strength makes up the difference.

Enkidu tosses a shoulder at Gilgamesh's jaw and Gilgamesh bites him. They roll in the dirt, both clenched too tightly to strike a good punch. Instead, they grab at each other's arms and fingers, trying to pull them the wrong way.

Some of the eunuchs from Inanna join with the women and boys, keeping the soldiers at bay. Shamhat takes note of which ones came to her aid, and which ones did not.

The wedding party is over. A few of the guests stand at a distance watching the fight. It's exciting to see someone challenge the king. The fighting men rise up from the dirt in a clench and the onlookers cheer. Gilgamesh tries to free an arm to swing, but Enkidu twists him back to the ground. The fight rolls across the street and spectators jump out of the way. Slowly the crowd begins to thin — this is exciting, but it's safer at home.

Time drags on and the fight is moving slower. Neither Gilgamesh nor Enkidu is winning. The men's muscles tense and pull but each effort meets its equal. The fight is more exertion than movement. It gets late and after a while, everyone has gone home. Even the soldiers and eunuchs appear to have gone to tend their wounds.

Shamhat waits with the father-in-law; he brought beer and warm broth and they watch from the house.

As the blue before dawn creeps up the horizon, Enkidu and Gilgamesh stand, teeth on each other's trapezius, throwing the occasional wobbly punch. Then they both tilt to the side, falling away from each other and crumpling to the street. Neither of them moves.

Shamhat quickly thanks her host and goes to check that the men are still breathing. Six of Gilgamesh's soldiers appear out of the shadows and shove her aside. Shamhat yells and wakes up one of the temple eunuchs crouched against the side of the house.

Two of the soldiers are carrying weapons and they face Shamhat and the eunuch. The other soldiers pair up and lift Gilgamesh and Enkidu, putting arms around their shoulders to drag them away. The eunuch stares at the soldier in front of him and begins tensing forward. The soldier puts his spear tip at the base of the eunuch's neck. Shamhat grips the eunuch's wrist.

The soldier facing the eunuch waits a short time after Gilgamesh and Enkidu have been dragged away, then steps back and pivots his spear to jam the butt end at the eunuch's chest. He looks the eunuch hard in the eye, then he and the other soldier turn and march toward the palace.

Shamhat runs back to the temple and calls for the boy.

She sends him to the palace to see if he can get any news.

— 3 —

Enkidu awakes flat on his back in a small room. His feet are up against a wall, his head touching the wall opposite. The fingers of his left hand feel wood, he turns his head and peels one eye open. There is a large wooden door with a smaller door set into it at about standing eye level. His neck isn't broken.

He flexes his hands. They're painful, but mostly still working. Swollen, bloody patches, a couple of sprains. His right little finger is pointing out at a bad angle.

He slowly bends his wrists, elbows, and shoulders and they are still working. He reaches over and yanks his little finger straight. The sharp pain causes him to cough, and he can feel some cracked ribs. He will wait until later to find out how many.

The ringing in his head is getting louder. Or maybe he is just becoming more fully awake. He tries moving his mouth and eyebrows and there is a flood of pain. They are too beat up to give any useful information. His tongue is swollen solid, a sharp ache mixed with blood. He'll have to check his teeth later. He flexes an ankle, hip, and knee, and first one leg then the other.

Nothing seriously broken, but the pain from everywhere is rising. It will be a while before he knows the details. The room is too narrow to stretch both arms out straight, so he puts one hand on the door sill and the other on the wall opposite. He pulls up, steadying himself as he bends upward to a sitting position.

Nausea.

He hangs his head forward until it passes.

In the corner of the room by his left foot, he now sees a hole dug in the dirt floor, stinking of shit. There is a cluster of flies clinging to the walls above it. He is relieved that the smell wasn't coming from him. He lets the pain sink in. His breathing doesn't rattle very much at the moment. He's in pretty good shape, considering how he got here, wherever this is.

Ready to try standing, he braces his hands against the wall and lifts himself up. Knees are reluctant, but they'll hold for now. Taking the time to unbend his back, his broken ribs are still broken.

He keeps one hand on the wall as he surveys his room and lifts an arm upward. The ceiling is high enough that he couldn't put his hand flat on it, even if his ribs would let him try.

Everything is dingy plastered mud-brick except for the door. He knocks on it to judge its thickness, maybe as much as his wrist. At this, the small door opens and there is a face looking in. He recognizes the leather headgear of Gilgamesh's soldiers.

Twice a day the guard brings a ration of flat bread and beer. The guard opens the small door and puts them on the ledge. Enkidu knows the daytime by the thin light seeping under his door. He guesses the passage of days by the level in his shit hole.

The guard doesn't speak and Enkidu doesn't call him. His wounds are healing but his ribs still hurt if he isn't careful how he moves. He can use his tongue now, he only lost one of his front teeth.

Enkidu amuses himself by pushing his feet against one narrow wall and his back against the other, then shifting one foot to the near wall and lifting himself up. His ribs complain if he moves too quickly.

— 4 —

Then one day: banging on the door.

Enkidu slides down from his perch near the ceiling. He crouches ready in the corner behind the door hinge. The door opens and a bronze spearpoint pokes through. Enkidu grabs the spear by the shaft and yanks it away from its owner. He knocks the door fully open and shoves the butt of the spear into the soldier's belly.

But there are more soldiers. Two of them grab the spear shaft as Enkidu lunges out of the cell. Another soldier tosses a stout rope around him and two more pull it tight. They tie his arms to his torso and somehow manage to bind his ankles. One of the soldiers gets kicked in the jaw. The soldiers with the rope yank him down and start dragging him over the stone floor. The other soldiers follow behind.

Enkidu decides it's useless to struggle. Instead, he feels for a loose place in the rope and a knot he can reach. He has to lift his head as they drag him up the stairs. Then they turn down another corridor. They enter a room draped in curtains of lush purple with gold thread woven in.

Gilgamesh sits at the end of the room, in a large wooden chair whose arms are carved like lion paws. It has lion haunches for feet, and a lion head carved in relief on the back, all leafed with gold, and inlaid with lapis lazuli.

Enkidu notices that they've straightened Gilgamesh's nose. The scars on the king's face are healing, but Gilgamesh hasn't risen from his chair, so Enkidu can't tell what other injuries he might have. The soldiers drag Enkidu up to a few paces from Gilgamesh, he lifts his hand and the soldiers drop the rope and back away.

Gilgamesh looks at Enkidu there on the floor. He's smiling, Enkidu sees that the king has all his teeth.

Gilgamesh looks like he is enjoying himself, and he speaks, "Hey wild man, you put up a pretty good fight, but you admit that I won, don't you? And thanks for coming up to see me, I was wondering how you were doing. I see that you're all healed up, so now we can get down to business."

Enkidu says nothing, watching Gilgamesh's face.

"What do you say, wild man? We could have some adventures, you and me. If you feel like cooperating."

Gilgamesh looks around the room.

"Does he even know what I'm saying? Does anyone here talk wild man language?"

Gilgamesh remains seated, watching Enkidu hog-tied on the floor, while a skinny errand boy runs to find a soldier to translate. When the translator arrives it only makes things worse. He translates into a dialect from east of the Tigris, one that Enkidu barely recognizes.

Gilgamesh is talking about plans for an expedition far into the mountains, between Mari and Ebla, to the great cedar forests on the upper Euphrates.

"Do you know the way there, wild man? Can you lead us overland, not following the river? It'll be an adventure, we'll go through the wild lands and not see the cities. Didn't you come from around there, wild man?"

Gilgamesh has stopped talking, it looks like he expects a response. Enkidu has been to the edge of one of the cedar forests, but he knows nothing of Mari or Ebla. How much does the tyrant know about him? Does he know anything or is he just talking? Enkidu sees no advantage in giving Gilgamesh any information, so he answers using his worst city language, sounding like a child with a thick accent.

"I know the place. But why should I?"

Gilgamesh's face brightens like a boy winning a game. Hearing Enkidu's challenge, he glances over to his soldiers, grinning like he knows he can't lose.

"Well, wild man, pick yourself up and lead us to the cedars, then I'll untie your rope."

The soldiers laugh. They find Gilgamesh quite funny.

"Maybe if you lead us there and don't run away, then I'll set you free. Or instead, if you don't cooperate, then maybe I'll kill you. Swear your allegiance and I'll have them untie your feet."

Enkidu glares at him, "King, why not throw me back in that cell? You only offer to give back something you've stolen."

Gilgamesh laughs and turns to his soldiers, and then they laugh too.

"Ah! Wild man, you are more clever than I expected! Already you understand how it is to be king. You can go back to your cell. Take a few days to consider your choices. Will you swear allegiance or do the guards drag you?"

Enkidu looks Gilgamesh straight in the eye, "King, if you want me to bow down to you, then they can drag me. But if they untie me, I will not fight. Unless you break your word."

Gilgamesh didn't think that was funny. His face turns sour.

"Take him away," he says, tossing his hand.

The guards drag Enkidu back to his cell. Standing him up, they half loosen the knot on his hands, push him inside, and bolt the door.

A few days later the guards come to Enkidu's room. They tie his hands at his sides, and he doesn't fight them. They walk in front and behind him up to the throne room.

Gilgamesh says, "Hey wild man, feeling a little tamer now, are you? That's good, but don't take the tameness too far, or you won't be any fun anymore. But now that you're getting a little civilized, me and you could have a good time. I heard that you were starting to like it here in Uruk. Didn't you have a girlfriend over at the temple? You like our city women better than your hairy wild girls? But never mind that, let's talk about our adventure. Are you ready to lead us to the cedar forest yet? How long will it take us to get there?"

Enkidu waits to see if Gilgamesh is finished before he answers. This king is an unruly child, what reason could there be to play along with his games? But nothing about this situation makes any sense. Except that Gilgamesh has him locked in a cage.

Even so, he feels the ground slowly shifting, tilting toward Gilgamesh. Enkidu hears himself say, "I can lead you to the cedar forest. If we left now and moved quickly, the journey would probably take from this new moon until about the new moon after the next one."

"Excellent!" Gilgamesh smiles, "I'll have my man assemble our party and provisions. Fifty men should do, I think, and some porters and servants and some other details."

"More than fifty men, you say?" Enkidu shakes his head. "That's different. Fifty men are too many to feed themselves from the land as they go. There will not be enough game for such a large number. You'll need to carry much of your food along with you. That's not how my people travel. I don't know how to provide for so many men walking. Having such a large party will make the travel time much longer."

Gilgamesh says, "I thought you knew how to travel in the wilderness, wild man, but it sounds like all you know how to do is waste time wandering around. But no matter, my captain will figure out how to handle the provisions, all you need to do is show us the way."

Gilgamesh's face brightens, "So we have a deal, then? You'll show us the way to the cedar forest? Tell me you are with us and I'll get you a better place than that jail cell."

Enkidu shrugs, "I will not fight you, king. I will lead you to the forest"

Enkidu's new room is much the same as the jail cell, but slightly larger, and the door isn't bolted. Down a corridor is a latrine and a bath that is shared by all the soldiers. They have stopped staring at Enkidu and now they mostly ignore him. Except sometimes as he passes by they make a grunting noise at him, a rude joke about his wild animal language.

Enkidu spends most of his time walking around the palace grounds, noticing the ways of the soldiers and workers and aristocrats. Now and then, one of Gilgamesh's guards will collect him and bring him to the king's rooms. Gilgamesh hasn't challenged Enkidu since their big fight, now he seems to be going out of his way to be friendly.

Sometimes they play the pebble game, making wagers with silver beads that Gilgamesh pours out of a deerskin bag. Sometimes they throw a large heavy ball back and forth, chanting a child's skipping tune faster and faster.

Sometimes Gilgamesh wants Enkidu to sit with him while he drinks beer and talks about his adventures. One time Enkidu drank beer too, and they sang together, simple songs with many verses. They told jokes and laughed. The beer made Gilgamesh funnier and more relaxed. Another time they arm wrestled, ending by calling a draw. They haven't wrestled since.

Gilgamesh's provisioners are assembling a pack train. They have brought tents and cooks and servants and three months' worth of food. They need a hundred donkeys and dozens of drovers. The metal workers have made fifty bronze axes, and Gilgamesh has drafted fifty young men to wield them.

Enkidu shakes his head, remembering how little his family carried. If you are not in a hurry and know the land you are walking, there's no need to carry extra food. The land will provide as you go.

Normally, city people travel along the river, going from one city to the next. They get their meals and lodging from other city people along the way. This is a curious expedition Gilgamesh is making, going through the wild lands and carrying so many things.

Enkidu tells Gilgamesh that he can assist with provisioning the trip. There will not be enough game to feed the whole party, but there will be some, and if Enkidu has a bow for hunting, they could have better meat along the way.

Gilgamesh raises an eyebrow. "I didn't know you used real weapons, wild man. I thought you only used sticks and rocks. Let's see your skill with a bow. Guard, bring us bows and arrows, and set up targets out in the yard."

They bring two cloth bags, densely packed with straw. Both are painted with a white circle of four handbreadths and a black circle of one handbreadth at the center. Gilgamesh and Enkidu stand at twenty paces and shoot at the targets, five arrows each, and then they walk to the targets to check their marksmanship.

Gilgamesh loves to compete, and he is skilled with a bow. After the first five arrows, they go to the targets and see that both of them have hit four arrows in the black circle and one in the white.

Gilgamesh says, "But look, my four in the black are closer to the center than yours, and mine in the white is only barely outside the black."

They shoot again, this time from twenty-five paces. Gilgamesh shoots first, and they alternate shots until Enkidu shoots his fifth arrow. Then they put down their bows and walk to the targets. Enkidu reaches his target and checks his arrows, three in the black, and two in the white. Respectable, but not excellent. He looks at Gilgamesh's target and there are only two in the black.

But Gilgamesh isn't standing there beside him. He is back at the shooting line, and he looses another arrow. Enkidu feels its wind and the thunk of impact as the arrow hits the black circle of the target. Gilgamesh shouts, "There! See? We're even! We both got three in the black."

Enkidu doesn't answer. He will remember to not take his eyes off Gilgamesh again.

But Gilgamesh seems to be in a cheerful mood. He makes a show of presenting the bow and arrows to Enkidu as a gift. "I didn't know you were such a fine bowman, wild man. You deserve to have a well-made bow like this one. Also, come with me to my storehouse, we'll get you a decent knife so you can dress the game you kill."

Gilgamesh presents the knife to Enkidu, sharp polished bronze with an oiled wooden handle and a leather sheath for carrying it. Then he stands back to watch Enkidu's appreciation of his generosity. Enkidu holds the knife in his hand. It is well made, nicely balanced, and the blade is sharp, but the bronze raises an unpleasant taste at the back of his tongue.

He nods to Gilgamesh, "Thank you, king, for these very fine gifts. I will try to make good use of them."

Enkidu visits the donkeys in the stables and strokes the coarse hair of their muzzles. He brushes the donkey's necks and backs and sides and sees their eyes soften and close. Their ears turn as he lightly sings a little song of the hillside after the rains, grown tall with new grass. He watches birds fly over the palace grounds and listens for news in their calls. He doesn't go near the soldiers guarding the gate, he will be out of here soon enough.

One day Enkidu sees Shamhat's boy unloading a donkey cart loaded with cheese. The boy sees him and Enkidu nods. He waits until no one else is around, then comes up to the boy. Enkidu asks if there has been any news of Ninsigal. The boy lifts his hands and shakes his head 'no.'

Enkidu tells the boy that he will be going northwest to the cedar forest. Maybe he can share that news with Shamhat. At the mention of her name, the boy dips his head and gives a faint smile. The cheese man is coming back with an empty basket, and Enkidu wanders aimlessly away.

Gilgamesh and his captains have been staying on the palace grounds. They do nothing but talk of the cedar forest campaign, they don't even go into the city to cause their usual trouble. And wherever he goes, Gilgamesh is trailed by richly dressed men trying to get his attention.

One time when Enkidu is nearby, Gilgamesh sees him and calls him over. "Hey wild man, come over here and meet some of my friends."

Enkidu comes closer, and Gilgamesh throws an arm around his neck.

"See this, men? He's my wild man. He's going to show us around the boondocks on the way to the cedar forest."

Enkidu doesn't reply to Gilgamesh and shrugs loose from under his arm. He stands and watches the men's faces as they look him over. These are the men Shamhat described when she was talking about men who had slave girls. Or men just like these, anyway. One of these men standing in front of him might have Ninsigal in a cage.

A thought: why not just ask them? "Hey king, I've heard that some of you keep slave women for yourselves. What about your friends here? Have any of them gotten a new slave girl lately?"

Gilgamesh puts his arm back around Enkidu's neck, tighter this time, and he laughs. "Ha! Yes, it's true, these friends of mine are masters with women. Why? Are you looking for a girlfriend?"

The king's mouth is still smiling but his eyes have turned cold. He releases Enkidu's neck and turns back to his friends. The king and the men walk away, returning to their conversation as if nothing had happened.

At night in the palace, the men feast and drink and accost a room full of naked women. One night Gilgamesh finds Enkidu and drags him to the party, pulling him by the hand into the dining hall, up to the front of the room.

Gilgamesh quiets the crowd and begins speaking, telling a story about the wild man. "He had been just like another wild animal running with the gazelle. And then he was seduced by the prostitute and she brought him to the city. She cut his hair and taught him to eat human food. And then after I beat him in our epic fight, see how tame he looks now? Yes, it's true, but he only looks tame on the outside, he's still nearly as wild as he was."

"All that wild man power is still in him, and we share it, him and me. Look at how close we are — just like brothers. I'm feeling a little wild myself right now."

Gilgamesh holds Enkidu's hand up above their heads and the room rumbles, the nobles speaking low to each other, not sure whether to cheer or be worried.

Gilgamesh releases Enkidu's hand and lifts a cup of beer to toast the forest adventure. The room starts getting louder, and Enkidu slips away to the banquet table. He picks up a joint of roast gazelle and a little delicacy they've made from the starchy reed tubers his family collects as a staple.

The men are getting drunker and they've started pulling at the serving girls' aprons. Gilgamesh nods to a servant, and the courtesans are brought in.

They saunter in one by one, pause in the doorway to do a little tease of pulling open their robes, then come into the room, slipping the robes off their shoulders to drop them in a pile by the door.

Musicians have started playing louder, and the courtesans sway to the rhythm, they toss their heads back, loose hair falling down their shoulders, wave their hands in the air, and rock their bare hips.

Gilgamesh catches one of the women by the hand and pulls her in front of himself, pressing her backside to his thighs. He reaches around and lifts her breasts in his hands, then walks her right up to Enkidu.

Before Enkidu can move away, Gilgamesh drops one of the breasts and catches him by a wrist, pulls him tight, and hugs the woman between them, her face in Enkidu's chest. Gilgamesh leans over toward Enkidu's face. He puts on a leering grin, then puckers his lips and makes a wet noise.

Enkidu twists his wrist loose and pushes Gilgamesh's other hand from behind him. He steps back, holds the woman by her shoulders, and scans her face from arm's length. Her eyes are obscured by heavy-painted lids. The red smile on her lips is saying something different from her body.

Her perfume doesn't fully cover a stale sour scent.

Enkidu can smell the place where her oiled skin smudged onto his chest. He looks Gilgamesh hard in the eye and shakes his head. Gilgamesh makes a laugh as if he doesn't care, but behind the eyes is a look Enkidu has seen before, one time he'd wrestled a young bully too quickly to the ground.

Enkidu lets go of the woman's shoulders and turns, pushing through the crowd, leaving Gilgamesh with the woman. He's had many nights alone together with Shamhat, this crowd of noisy grown children makes him feel more ill than aroused.

The nobles and hangers-on have gotten sloppy drunk and started dropping their clothing. The soldiers sit around the edges of the room looking sullen and drinking.

The next day Enkidu goes to the clothing storehouse, finds a sheepskin skirt, and puts it on.

— 6 —

The caravan starts out from the palace gate at first light, Gilgamesh and Enkidu at the lead. Gilgamesh walks tall, the king going out on a mission. Enkidu follows a little behind him, scanning the faces of the crowd along the road.

There are musicians blowing horns and beating silver cymbals, aggravating the hangovers of the soldiers and drovers. It is the heat of the day before the whole procession has lined up and gotten through the west gate of the city. It takes the rest of the day just to get them all across the river.

Enkidu is supposed to be guiding them, but the second day is nothing more than going back out the same road he'd been on the day he first came to Uruk. But Gilgamesh is having an adventure, and he puts on his royal visage for the farmers they pass, draws his sword, and spread his arms wide.

Enkidu is finding his bearings, walking west away from the river. They will still follow the river more or less but keep some distance to avoid the cities.

By the fourth day, the road has turned into multiple goat paths, though Enkidu has a good sense of which path to take. He has begun to recognize the foxtail barley and slender oats standing ripe on the hills.

The men are already bored. Gilgamesh has stationed soldiers at the rear of the train to prevent more men from deserting.

Enkidu is glad to have his feet back on living soil. In the city, he had gotten out of the habit of noticing the feel of the ground. He remembers a song that fits this path and sings it quietly to himself. He sings for the grouse trails and lizard holes and wildcat scat. The scent of wormwood on the breeze comes down a fold in the hills.

Keeping his eyes open for signs of his people, he longs to see even their footprints. But he must not let this caravan of rabble get anywhere near them. There is so much to look at he scarcely hears the men complain about the heat and the dirt and the food and no women. Gilgamesh still carries himself as if he is having an adventure, but now with no roadside admirers to impress, he turns to Enkidu instead.

Gilgamesh points to the grassy slope ahead of them, "Hey wild man, I heard you were good at catching gazelle. Why don't you go get one, and we'll have a feast tonight. Or do they all run away from you now?"

Gilgamesh pulls a stalk of yarrow from beside the trail, "Hey wild man, is this one of the plant leaves you used to eat? Show me the roots and grubs you eat too. That way if we run out of barley we won't need to starve. The cooks could make some wild man food. Or maybe you and me could stay out here forever, and I could be the king of the beasts."

Gilgamesh leans in close to Enkidu as they walk, and in a low voice, he says "Hey wild man, I heard about you and that girl Shamhat. She must be pretty good, eh? Is she the one that made you too picky for the palace girls? I'll have to go visit her when we get back."

Enkidu says that hunting gazelle is a good idea. He'll scout up ahead and look around. See which way to turn when they come to that next hill, leave a trail mark, then go look for game.

Gilgamesh sends a soldier to watch Enkidu as he walks, and that is what he does, nothing but walk. Gilgamesh sends a soldier the next time too, and the time after that, but now the soldiers just toss their heads, nothing suspicious ever happens and there isn't any place to run away to anyway, it's all just a vast nowhere of dirt and weedy bushes. So Gilgamesh stops sending the soldiers.

Enkidu scouts ahead for a little while nearly every day. He will bend a branch by the trail, or stack some rocks at a fork. This gets him away from the pack train, and Gilgamesh can act like a pathfinder, reading Enkidu's signs. And once in a while he gets lucky, there is a deer or a partridge that hasn't heard the rabble parade coming, and Enkidu can bring back fresh meat.

Gilgamesh smiles when Enkidu brings back game to the caravan. He slaps Enkidu's back and calls him "The Hunter." He praises Enkidu to the cooks and gives them instructions on how to prepare the game and which of the men to give the choice cuts.

One day Enkidu sees the signs of a nomad campsite a little way off the trail. He's excited and afraid and happy all at once. He is walking up ahead of the pack train. The land has gotten rougher, they are gaining some elevation. The donkeys are moving more slowly.

Thankfully, this means he has some time before they catch up. Enkidu keeps walking, marking the trail for Gilgamesh. Then he doubles back off the trail, through the bushes to the nomad camp. He is careful to not break any twigs or let the fleece of his skirt catch. He wipes out his footprints in the soft places.

The children see him coming and they run away from the big man wearing city clothing. Enkidu sings his greeting, announcing his name and his family. The women start shouting "Enkidu is back from the dead!" as he hurries toward them, quickly asking them to be quiet, so he can tell his story and they will know what danger is coming their way.

He leaves out many of the details because there isn't much time, but when they hear his story, they are amazed at his travels, and he can't even begin to answer all of their questions.

These are his cousins, because all of them are cousins, but this band is the families of his mother's mother's younger brother's wife, together with the wife's sister's family. They assure Enkidu that at the next seasonal meeting, they will tell his father and uncle that they have seen him, and tell everyone about his amazing journey to Uruk and how he lived in the temple with a priestess and traveled with the king.

Enkidu has to interrupt their questions about his adventures. He tells them that he needs to hurry. Then he asks if they have seen any evidence of Ninsigal from after she was kidnapped.

None of them has any news of Ninsigal, but there is one of the young cousins, his beard barely filled in, who had seen three soldiers a few months ago walking with a loaded donkey. It was far from any place that soldiers would normally go, about two days northwest of the seed grass hills, it was only those three men, around the full moon after the one when Enkidu started walking to Uruk.

After he tells the news, the young man holds Enkidu's eye for a moment, then after a glance to his mother and aunts, he drops his eyes, and almost as if to himself he says, "Maybe someday we will start defending ourselves."

The young men have seen Gilgamesh's caravan coming, and they've been spying on it for the last two days as it approached their camp. They recognized those same three soldiers walking close together toward the rear of the train. The soldiers' skirts are faded to pink and dirtier than the others, but their spear points are very shiny, two young ones with brown hair and the other one older and bald. The bald one has a fresh scar from his left cheek to his ear.

Enkidu thanks them for that information and asks them what they know of the way to the cedar forests.

These cousins have been there, and they describe the way to the forest, giving Enkidu some landmarks to watch for.

"But what is the king planning to do at the cedar forest with such a big crowd?" They ask him, "Surely Gilgamesh doesn't believe he can steal timber from Ebla without anyone noticing. And it is a bad idea anyway, the timberlands are drying the same as the grasslands. Even now there are many bare weedy places where trees were cut and the forest isn't growing back."

Enkidu knows the story doesn't make sense yet. Maybe it never will. This seems to be how it is with kings. He wishes that he could see these cousins again afterward and tell them how it turns out. But right now he must go, and they need to disappear as quickly as possible.

Enkidu kisses his cousins, thanks them again for their news, and picks his way back to the trail.

Now when he goes out ahead of the caravan, the first thing he does is find a blind where he can watch the soldiers as they pass. He notices how the various soldiers walk in their groups, and he finds the three men his cousins identified. He watches those three men as they lean in to talk with each other as they walk. He watches them as they share a sharp laugh at a joke that the older man told. In the city, these men could easily lose him if they ran, but here in the wilds, if they left the train he'd have no trouble tracking them.

One evening, the train crests a ridge and they make camp with a broad view of the valley ahead. That night, before dawn, as the eastern horizon is just starting to lighten, Enkidu comes awake to see Gilgamesh entering his tent.

"Hey wild man, I had a dream and it woke me up. You know about dream things, so tell me what this means. I had arrived at the cedar forest, up ahead there was a big mountain. I felt happy and strong. Then there was a loud roar, the mountain rose up and fell on me, and then I woke up."

Enkidu leans up on his elbow. "I don't know what that means. But having a mountain fall on you doesn't sound like a good thing."

"Maybe, but I'm still alive and standing here, aren't I? What if the mountain was my enemies, and this means they couldn't defeat me?"

Enkidu doesn't answer, just shrugs and lies back down on his mat. Gilgamesh stands for a long moment looking at Enkidu, his arms folded on his chest. Then lets his hands drop and turns to duck back out of the tent.

They break camp in the morning and make their way downhill into the valley, pushing across the creek by midday, and then climb up the far slope just before sunset. Here, too, when they crest the ridge they see another valley ahead of them.

And again, in the middle of the night, Gilgamesh wakes Enkidu and tells him a dream.

"I had another dream. This time as I arrived at the cedar forest, there was a storm with lightning, and that set the mountain on fire, then the mountain rose up and fell on me, but the rain started and it poured down and the mountain was washed away by a flood. What do you think that means, wild man?"

Enkidu says, "I told you I don't know about your dreams. Why don't you have your ministers tell you, isn't that what you keep them for?"

"Well, yes, that is their job," says Gilgamesh, "but none of my ministers wanted to come along on this trip, so why don't you tell me instead?"

Enkidu pretends to look serious, "Mm, that doesn't surprise me. This dream sounds a lot like the other one. Why don't you just take it to mean the same thing, whatever that was?"

Gilgamesh says, "That's a good idea wild man. I will be victorious. Thanks."

⫞⟠◇

One morning Enkidu and Gilgamesh are walking side by side a little ahead of the parade. Both of them see the signs, and they grab at each other's arms and point.

Enkidu sees a hoof print, and Gilgamesh points to a pile of dung. An auroch passed by here, and not long ago! The tracks cross their path then head uphill toward a fold in the hillside to the west.

The hoof prints are large, made by only one animal. A bull traveling alone. Without further thought the two men run after it, checking the tracks in the sand and the broken twigs beside the trail.

Another pile of dung, and this one still warm, the tracks lead toward a patch of willows in a hollow place on the hill, it looks like a water hole. Lucky that the breeze is blowing toward them and won't carry their scent.

Enkidu takes his bow from his shoulder and nocks an arrow, Gilgamesh pulls his sword loose from his belt, slowly, quietly.

Enkidu looks to Gilgamesh and puts a hand on his arm: they must not let the auroch hear them approach. They crouch through the willows until there is only one line of trees between them and the water hole. They see a great bull, he is facing slightly away from them, bending down to drink from a little pool among the rocks. Enkidu watches the auroch as he laps at the water in the pool, the tail swishing at flies, ears swiveling to the warning sounds of the birds in the willows.

But the bull has not startled at the presence of men. Enkidu takes time to see the auroch, then aims his arrow, draws back, and shoots, hitting the bull's rib above his heart. Then quickly another arrow nocked and aimed as the bull jerks up his head to find his attacker. The arrow catches at an angle in the bull's neck just above his throat.

The auroch shakes and bellows, looking in their direction, doesn't appear to see them, but runs straight at them anyway. The bull crashes through the willows, breaking branches in the way, so close that Enkidu can smell the bull's breath as a sapling whips his face.

Gilgamesh is behind Enkidu, and he leaps up, dodging between the wide horns, driving his sword deep into the base of the bull's neck. The auroch's front legs buckle and his chest hits the ground, he snorts and swings his head as the men roll out of the way.

Enkidu clambers up from the ground, facing the bull, just out of reach of the horns. He catches the animal's eye, black and fierce. The auroch snorts once, then again, as if taking the man's measure.

The bull's breathing slows a little, thick neck muscles loosen, settling the head to the ground.

Enkidu holds the animal's eye, and says "Thank you, brother." Then he steps onto the bull's horn on the ground and pulls on the other horn that points upward. He leans back, twisting the bull's head around to the side. Gilgamesh gets to his feet, pulls his sword from the bull's neck hump, and reaches around to slice the bull's throat. Dark blood spurts from the artery and the light drains from the auroch's eye.

The men drop their weapons, and slap each other in a bloody embrace, a well-played hunt and such a glorious bull! Then each man grabs a hind leg at the fetlock, tugging the hindquarters uphill of the head so the beast will bleed out. Enkidu trots back to the caravan to get some men to help butcher their kill and carry back the meat.

The train stops for the day and the cooks make a feast. Gutting and skinning and cutting up the carcass. Collecting rocks to build a trench fire pit. The ax men scout for firewood and spits for the roasting. The drovers carry baskets of butchery waste away from camp and fling them into the bushes.

Gilgamesh presents the heart, tongue, and liver to his officers and favorites. He holds up their hands and makes a little speech, spreading the glory among his men. Then they draw lots, gambling for who gets to keep the hide. There is roast meat for everyone, and the men spend the rest of the day eating and lounging. Gilgamesh lifts the heavy bull head above him, laughs, and tells a story praising Enkidu the great hunter. Enkidu notices how everyone is happy when Gilgamesh is feeling generous.

The next day the men are in a better mood, and the pack train makes good distance. They set up camp on a grassy sloping plain which is cut by a creek bed. There are small pools where the creek bed is deep and shaded. The air is cooler here, a little higher elevation, and the days starting to get shorter.

The cooks serve up more auroch meat, and all of them eat their fill.

After dark, Enkidu is lying on the mat in his tent, nearly asleep.

Gilgamesh ducks through the flap and comes into the tent. He lies down beside Enkidu, then puts his hand on Enkidu's thigh, slides the hand down Enkidu's skirt, and reaches inside.

Enkidu turns and puts his hand up Gilgamesh's skirt, grips him tight, and gives him a sharp twisting yank.

"Ow!" Gilgamesh yelps and scrambles to his feet. "What did you do that for, wild man?"

"You may be king," says Enkidu, "but I'm not one of your slave girls."

Gilgamesh pouts, "Hey wild man, it's not like that. I thought we were friends."

Enkidu reminds him, "Have you forgotten the first time I saw you? When you were trying to rape that new husband's wife?"

"Oh, that." Gilgamesh shrugs. "That was a long time ago, and I haven't raped any virgin brides since then. And besides, I'm the king, people expect me to do that kind of thing."

Enkidu turns away, "I don't know what your people expect, but my people don't want to be treated that way. We don't have kings, and maybe that's the reason. Maybe because we expect them to act just like you do."

Gilgamesh humphs. "You're probably one of those soft boys who can only have sex with women."

Enkidu takes a breath, "Listen, king, you're not going to get what you want by insulting me. Just go away, and I'll let you know if I change my mind."

Gilgamesh mumbles, "Or maybe you're still in love with that temple prostitute."

Enkidu doesn't respond to that, and eventually, Gilgamesh slinks out of the tent.

⚜◈◇

Late one morning a day or two later, Enkidu and Gilgamesh are walking at the front of the caravan, and Enkidu asks Gilgamesh, "Hey king, why do you suppose the people of Uruk tolerate you being king?"

Gilgamesh lets out a laugh, and speaks to Enkidu as if he's a child, "Because I am the king."

Enkidu nods his head, "Yes, I know that. And I understand the benefit your soldiers and your nobles get from you. But from what I saw in Uruk, most of the people don't get anything at all. Nothing good, anyway. Most of the people you just take things from. And you take so much, that a lot of them are struggling just to keep on living."

Gilgamesh frowns, "Well, I don't know how a wild man got to be such an expert on the social affairs of my city, but if the people are so miserable they can always leave and go someplace else. I am the king, and the people love their king. They love me, and surely you can see why they would. But besides that, the people understand that they need a king to make them great."

Gilgamesh puts his hand on his chest. "Uruk would not be a great city without me. It would just be some ordinary place where people lived and worked and traded their handiwork, or did whatever things they do, and pretty soon some other king would come and conquer them and they would all be slaves, or worse."

Enkidu lets out a breath, "Yes king, I understand that the other kings are a problem too. But isn't it better if most of the people feel satisfied with their lot in life? You make it sound like it's easy for people to go to a new place and start over. From what I have seen, once they have settled it looks really hard to pick up and go somewhere else."

"Well, then I don't see what the problem is." Gilgamesh spreads his hands, "Cities have kings. I am king of Uruk, and the people of

Uruk live as good a life as anybody else. Are you suggesting that they should all run off and be wild men?"

Enkidu looks at the ground, "No, that wouldn't work." He falls silent.

Gilgamesh pats his back and gives him a fatherly smile, as if he had just explained an adult topic to his young son.

Another day, Enkidu and Gilgamesh are sitting at the edge of camp eating their morning meal of barley cakes and dried meat, when Enkidu hears a bird call. He asks Gilgamesh, "Do you know that bird, the barley sparrow?"

Gilgamesh cocks his ear, then Enkidu points the direction of the call when it comes again. The bird sings "chee chee-chee-ch-ch-ch-ch-ch-chu-chu-chwee."

Gilgamesh shakes his head. "No, I don't know that bird."

Enkidu tells him, "It's a small brown bird. It has a pale grey collar and breast, and a fluttery way of flying. It eats the barley grains when they get ripe in early summer. I'm sure your farmers know about this bird. They can come in large flocks to feast on the fields of grain.

"But there was a time long ago before any of your farmers plant-ed their fields or dug their irrigation ditches." Enkidu's hands move with the flow of his story. "In those days, as the barley sparrows flew from one patch of ripening grain to another, our grandmoth-ers would follow them. When the women saw barley sparrows land at a patch of wild grain, they would wait and watch. They kept enough distance that the birds would not be scared away, happily eating the barley.

"Then after a while the women would sing the birds' greeting song. They'd ask to join them at the patch of grain, announcing themselves, asking to share the harvest. A skilled singer could hold the birds' attention from flying until they were almost within hand's reach.

Enkidu pauses for a moment with his hand extended before he continues. "This way the birds came to know that the people were also harvesters of grain. But not only harvesting. The women who threshed and cooked the barley also saved some seed. Then they spread that seed in other places that had the feel of the places the birds had shown them. These new places the women remembered, so they didn't need the birds to lead them. But the birds also learned to watch the women during grain harvest time. They would follow the women to the new patches."

He goes on, "The birds and the women knew each other, just like cousins. They remembered how they helped each other at harvest time. And then, after many years of planting the largest seeds in the best places, the little wild barley began changing into the fat, long barley that the farmers grow now."

Enkidu spreads his hands, "Maybe the birds don't remember those old days anymore, but our grandmothers pass down this story to us, and they don't complain when the birds take their share of the grain. They worked together for many generations.

Enkidu turns back to Gilgamesh, "Do you think your farmers know this story? Or do they see the sparrows only as a nuisance?"

Gilgamesh shrugs. "That's a nice story, wild man, but I haven't had any farmers tell me what they think about birds."

— 7 —

They have walked west, then northwest, west again, northwest, west, and now they are going northwest again. The food supplies are lighter now and the donkeys can walk faster, especially if they get good forage and water when they stop at the end of the day. And the men who go hunting for game along the trail have gotten lazy and started bringing some of the unladen donkeys to the cooks for slaughter.

Soon they will turn northward, putting Emar to their south, then move closer to the river where the forests will begin, a little south of Carchemish.

Climbing to crest a hill, the caravan sees in front of them a valley filled with trees. Scrubby and thin on the near down-slope, but by the bottom of the valley the creek bed is barely visible through the branches, and the far up-slope is thick with timber.

They skirt the valley downhill to the northeast, then cross the mostly dry creek and make their camp not far from the great river. The men are standing taller, they look up at the trees, eyes open wider. They forget to complain. Gilgamesh tells the cooks to give everyone an extra ration of beer. The men sleep that night under the trees, with the scent of cedar creeping into their dreams.

The next morning they break their traveling camp and climb up the hill, then downhill over the crest to the next creek where they set up their work camp and lay out their tools. Gilgamesh shouts for his men to gather around him, and he speaks, "They say that this forest is sacred, and that is true. They say that there are monsters here who will keep us from cutting the trees. But are we not strong men? Does anybody see a monster hiding in the trees? This morning this sacred forest will start serving the holy purpose of providing vast wealth for our city, and making all of us heroes."

The men cheer their king, and he leads the ax men up the hillside where they begin felling the cedar trees and stripping off their branches. The drovers and laborers drag the logs into piles beside the riverbank. Gilgamesh hustles from man to man, a slap to the shoulder and a quick bit of praise, a laugh about the big work ahead.

He takes the heaviest ax and sets to cutting trees, taunting the other ax men with the speed and power of his swing. They start with the trees at the top of the broad slope, then cut every tree all the way to the base of the valley and felling the trees up-slope. Making the drovers work quickly to get the fallen logs out of the way of the next tree being cut.

"Hey, wild man!" Gilgamesh shouts, "I bet I can cut a tree faster than you! Get an ax and race me."

"I'm sure you're right, king. I concede without contest." Enkidu tosses his hands. "I can use my talents better hunting for game."

"Good idea, wild man. And while you're at it, find me the biggest tree in the forest. We'll cut it down and be heroes."

Enkidu walks through the trees. On the hillside where the men are working, all the forest animals are in a panic. The birds are screeching, and the ground animals are gone. He walks up the creek, then over the ridge away from the pounding axes. There is no game to be found, all have run away from the noise. With nothing to hunt, Enkidu walks freely through the forest and marvels at this land. The creeks and steep slopes, trees blocking any long view. So different from the open, rolling savanna where he grew up.

Later, he is walking back to camp, a little up-slope from the creek, in the shadow of the trees, a thick layer of cedar needles cushions his footsteps. It is quiet, and the light is dimming, the birds have stopped their screeching. Maybe the sun has set, he can't be sure unless there is an opening where he can see up high enough to check for sunlight on the treetops. On the ground everything is shady, and most of the time he can't see much past the nearest tree trunks.

He steps over a large tree root and looks up. In front of him stands a massive tree. He walks up to it and leans his chest on the trunk, stretches his arms around it. His hands don't even reach halfway around. Looking up, he can't see how tall the tree is, the trunk disappears into a forest of branches above him. Only the lowest limbs are visible, closing the space between the surrounding trees.

Enkidu rests there with his chest against the tree, feels the pulse of his heart as his breath moves his body against the trunk, his fingers in fibrous grooves of bark. The only sound is from a light breeze on the treetops in the open sky high above, sight blocked by the branches overhead.

Then the wind shifts, bringing sounds from the logging camp in the distance. Thunk of ax and crack of timber, an occasional shout muffled through leafy woods.

Enkidu steps back, puts his hand on the trunk, and looks up.

He says "Good luck to you, grandmother," and makes his way back to camp.

After four days the ax men have cut a broad swath down the hillside, and they have begun to move up the next hill, while the soldiers and drovers hitch up donkeys and drag the logs to the river. They rope the logs together into wide rafts half floating in the shallows.

Enkidu goes walking in the woods every day, and when he returns to camp, Gilgamesh calls to him. "Hey wild man, what did you see out there in the woods? Me and my men made another great haul of timber today."

Gilgamesh smiles, happy when his boasting is true. "But I still need that greatest tree."

Enkidu shrugs, "There are so many trees. How could I say which is bigger than the next? Surely you have cut down some really big trees already."

It's true, Gilgamesh has cut down some big trees. He feels the power of his body and he can't get enough — swinging an ax at the tree, the flex of his muscles. His arm and the tool, back, shoulder, and leg all in one motion.

It is better than swinging a sword at an enemy. The tree is not an armed soldier, there is none of the danger-excitement of battle. A chance the tree might fall on him, a different flavor of danger, but still there is the muscle satisfaction of ax heft and impact. He can do this all day. The strength of his body bringing down tree after tree.

One afternoon Enkidu is walking in the woods and he comes upon a fresh deer sign, wet scat still warm, and new tracks in the leaf duff. He stops to listen. The deer is close enough that he can hear its rustling steps, foraging, not moving away. It's a young buck with his first little horns. Incautious and not listening, offering himself, he lets Enkidu sneak close enough to have a good shot, and so doesn't run far before he falls.

Enkidu heaves the deer onto his shoulders and carries it to camp. He brings it to the cooks and they are pleased with new meat. Then he walks to the creek to wash the deer blood from his hands and body.

Later, at the campfire, Gilgamesh wants to talk. He has eaten a good meal, and physical labor has made him calmer, he speaks more slowly, not as loud as before.

"Hey wild man, that was a nice deer you got, you're a pretty good hunter. But I'm curious, most of the time you aren't really hunting are you? I mean, isn't it more like you spend a lot of time wandering around, and then sometimes you happen across an animal that you can kill?"

Enkidu nods, perhaps a faint smile. "That's the way of it. I'd describe it a little differently, but yes, walking around with eyes open, and we see what there is."

"Okay, I think I know what you mean." Gilgamesh looks him in the eye. "But don't you ever feel like there is something bigger that you want to accomplish? Something more than wandering around and feeding yourself and picking up firewood? Like what me and my men are doing here in the forest, we're doing great work, and when we get home we'll be heroes, and people will tell stories about us. Isn't that what a man's life is for, doing something great that gets remembered?"

Enkidu is quiet for a little too long. Gilgamesh waits, his face open, like he has given Enkidu an important new idea.

Enkidu says, "My family is what I care about most. And thinking about what you said, I see that it is not any one great thing, but many small things that make a family. My people remember me because they love me, whether I do any great work or not. And I think I'd rather be happy than great. And now, when I say that, it makes me wonder what I am doing here, so far away from my family." Enkidu looks down at his hands, "I was going to be married."

Gilgamesh's eyes speak of kindness if not full understanding. He puts his arm around his friend, happy for someone to talk to.

— 8 —

The day comes when uncut trees are farther from the river, and the men have eaten the last donkey. There are trees they have cut, but without donkeys, they're too heavy to move. These they leave on the hillside where they fell. They've made a glorious haul already, and Gilgamesh decides there's no point in straining the men. He calls a halt to tree cutting, and they begin getting ready to break camp.

Gilgamesh goes down to the river the next morning. He calls to his men and they bring the skull of the auroch. Standing on the first log raft, he lifts the bull head onto a pole they've lashed to the front.

Gilgamesh shouts his glory.

The men raise their tools over their heads and cheer. The sun is high overhead before Gilgamesh wonders when he last saw Enkidu.

The three suspect soldiers have disappeared.

Enkidu circles the camp looking for them, stepping around the brush and refuse that line the edges of the camp. Since he'd seen those three the day before, they could not have gotten far. There doesn't appear to be anyone else looking for them, maybe nobody has noticed them gone.

Enkidu collects his travel kit and heads down to the river. He can't be certain, but he sees no sign of anyone having left the camp by water. So he walks along the bank through the river grass, downstream until he reaches uncut woods. Then he turns uphill and begins walking a loose circle beyond the slashed part of the forest, looking for signs of the three soldiers' trail.

When he crosses the caravan's path from Uruk he finds fresh tracks going back the way they came.

He doesn't see or hear the men but the signs say they're not far ahead. Tracking them, he gets closer as the day goes on. By dusk, the trees have thinned and the land has turned mostly to shrubs and grass.

Following the soldier's footprints, Enkidu hears them talking before he sees them. He slips off the trail to the cover of tall grass. The soldiers are making camp. Enkidu will wait.

The fall equinox has passed, and the moon is a little larger than its first quarter. Now it hangs just above the western horizon, telling Enkidu that he has waited more than half the night. He creeps up to the soldier's camp and stops at the edge of the circle of grass they have tramped down. The three of them are splayed out on the ground, asleep beside the embers of their campfire as if they have no concern for predators.

Enkidu stands still, watching the men as they sleep. It's a common enough sight but he can feel his gut begin to tighten and hear the thump of heartbeat rising to his ears. He sets down his travel kit and takes out Gilgamesh's bronze knife. Enkidu grips his knife and sees his next movements before the expanding rage can blind him.

Four long steps to the first one, bend, deep cut to neck and throat, turn without straightening, on to the next.

Killing men isn't the same as killing other animals. Just as he cuts their throats, each of the men wakes up confused. They swing their arms above their chests, hands gripping at nothing, choking on their own blood as they try to get to their feet.

The last of the three pauses in his body panic and catches Enkidu's eye. He looks like a young boy, wondering what the man is doing, then changes to adult surprise and fear when he begins to find out.

Enkidu's feet have to pull himself away from those eyes. He would have stood watching even after the man died.

Turning away from the camp, his heart pounding, Enkidu's rage leaks away, turning to nausea. He ducks back into the grass and picks up his kit. Runs the best he can until he buckles over. He vomits, kneeling with his face between open hands flat on the ground.

When the cold sweat has mostly settled, he pushes himself upright and gets away from that place as fast as he can. A hurried walk into full daylight, all the sensations passing through him, one to the next.

The satisfaction from killing vermin. Then the horror of the act. Simple heat of anger. Buzzing insect noise in his ears, with no sense or meaning. Amazement at power in his hands. And fear of what else they might do.

Who was he, who watched himself kill those three men? Those were not the actions of anyone he recognized. How will he explain this to his family?

All these come and go at their pace. They rise and linger and then begin to pass, washing through him until the sun is well beyond zenith. The sky is too bright. A thin white haze spreads the sunlight and makes him squint his eyes. He loosens his hair to let it fall across his face.

Then he falls into numbness.

He keeps walking.

Walking is only walking.

His feet are moving on the ground, but he isn't aware of any muscles working.

Then the numbness begins to fade. Relief at feeling the air in his lungs. Numbness takes time to clear, but the grief at the bottom will push through in due course.

Enkidu stops walking in early evening. He turns and sits with the sun at his back, feeling it warm him.

— 9 —

He walks for the next two days, only stopping to drink when he comes to a creek or a rock pool. His path has not crossed any human tracks from this season. He can finally breathe a little easier, beginning to feel some distance from those three dead men. But his body keeps reacting to the murder in cycles of sensations from that morning, feelings bleeding into memory and branching and reconnecting, all knitting themselves into his body.

At evening, he climbs a stony outcrop on a south-facing hill, sits and surveys the flattening slope below, chewing at the last piece of dried auroch in his kit. He must have dropped the knife on the night he killed those three soldiers.

There might be a grey streak in the hazy blue distance, perhaps some of his people have a campfire not too far from here. He notes the direction, then climbs down from the rock, into the grass a little way down the hill to make a nest for the night.

The next morning there is still a wisp of smoke hanging in the air over the plain below. Enkidu finds a deer trail that leads roughly in that direction. It takes him to a sandy stream bed which he follows toward the place he guesses the campfire had been.

Stopping to listen every few steps, the stream bank is too high for him to see over, but he hears movement above to his right. He slips farther from the water into taller rushes nearer the bank. Crouching down to disappear, he whistles a bird language greeting and waits for a reply.

Two whistled replies, sounding surprised. Enkidu climbs out of the stream bank and stands up above the grass. There he spots a pair of young men not far away. Enkidu sings his greeting, and the young men sing theirs back. They push their way through knee-high grasses and meet, clasping arms.

These young men have both taken the rites of adulthood but they are unmarried, traveling free of their parents' families. They can travel faster and farther, and they've set out to see the other sides of the familiar hills of their youth, perhaps see a little of the world where their families haven't been. They are traveling light, carrying only bows, a few arrows, a blanket, a fire kit, and a knife.

They are surprised to see someone traveling alone. This is unlucky and very unusual, and they are wary, wondering where Enkidu has been and what he is doing out here by himself. But they are curious to meet someone new.

These two are about Enkidu's age, perhaps a year younger, they call themselves Domun and Haladasi. Domun is shorter than Haladasi and quicker to talk. His face is round, his hands are quick, and he tends to laughter. Haladasi is thinner and more deliberate, considering his words before he speaks. The lines at his brow and the corners of his eyes have gotten ahead of his age.

Enkidu tells them that his story is long, and he will tell it to them. But he has just escaped from the king of Uruk, and he is on his way back to his own people.

Domun and Haladasi both look surprised at this, and they hurry through their formal introductions so they can hear the rest of Enkidu's story.

Each of the three men names their parents in turn, they follow their line until they find mutual cousins. They recall some of the seasonal meetings they've been to, and certain times when they had likely been there together, among the young boys running in packs. But they didn't grow up near each other. Domun and Haladasi's families traveled a circuit farther west and north from Enkidu's, they don't know very many people in common.

There is something else they need to know.

Enkidu stops, and says, "The night before two days past, I killed three of the king's soldiers."

The two young men's eyes go wide, and they take a step back and gape at the killer in front of them. The moment stretches, three men not moving, all attention to the eyes. Standing, still staring, after a while they begin to notice the heartbeat pulse in hands hanging at their sides, chests rising and falling with their breath, and the sharp edges of their vision beginning to haze.

Domun asks what happened.

Enkidu asks them if they knew anyone who'd been kidnapped.

They have both heard stories that a boy and a young woman suspiciously disappeared from a cousin's camp, but no one from either of their immediate families has been taken.

Enkidu nods and begins his story at the time when Ninsigal's father told them the news at the bush-apricot meeting. To tell the story, Enkidu starts walking in a circle around Domun and Haladasi at the center, and they have to keep turning to keep sight of him.

Enkidu tells the beginning, of Ninsigal being taken. Then the end, where he killed the three soldiers. He starts again at the beginning, telling the tale of his walk to the city and all that happened after.

Domun and Haladasi have started to walk behind Enkidu, following in his circle, and they are asking him questions about the path he took to the city and all that he saw and the soldiers and the rich men at the gate. Then Domun breaks from the circle and the others follow him and they are on the path to Domun and Haladasi's camp.

Haladasi has gotten a fire started, and they are sitting down. Enkidu gets to the part where he meets Shamhat. The young men grab his arms and interrupt him to make him tell again about meeting a Lady of the temple of Inanna at Uruk.

They want all the details of what she looked like and what she said and what they did together and more detail about what they did together, and the food that they ate. Then they make him tell it all one more time.

The telling has taken the whole day, getting mixed up because of all the interruptions and they haven't gone to find food. So they share a bunch of onion bulbs and carrot roots that Domun had cooked in the embers of last night's fire.

Enkidu tries to find some other detail that might make sense of how he got here. But then the words stop coming. He can't talk anymore, so they finally settle down for the night.

When they wake in the morning, Domun and Haladasi look at each other and remember about Enkidu killing the soldiers.

Enkidu is a big man and he has had some amazing adventures. But he doesn't look or act like a killer. Domun and Haladasi each imagine themselves doing some of the things Enkidu did. Still, they are a little spooked. They stand next to each other and look at the ashes of yesterday's fire.

Later in the morning, the three men go out looking for something to eat. They find a fig tree hanging with drying ripe fruit, and they eat their fill. Domun looks to Haladasi, and they agree that they are feeling a little better. They ask Enkidu again about the women of the city.

Domun and Haladasi are young men, full of inexperience and desire, they're not sure how to attract the attention of even their own sisters' friends. They are dazzled by Enkidu's story.

They smile to themselves and imagine loving a woman dressed in fine linen. They laugh and shake their heads, they can't believe that Enkidu walked through the gates of Uruk and into the temple of Inanna and loved a Lady of the temple.

To Enkidu, these two are just like his cousins. Just like his parents and uncles, for that matter. None of them has been inside the walls of the cities that press against the wild lands. But everyone tells stories about the cities. They pass them from hand to hand. Though nobody knows for sure who it was that went to the city and came back to tell those stories in the first place.

Enkidu wants to hear the news from Domun and Haladasi's families, along with the others of his people they know in common, but he will need to wait. They aren't much interested in talking about such ordinary things. They talk of Enkidu as if he is a hero from a legend, like the man who tricked the soldiers and stole the king's favorite sheep.

This reminds them about killing the three men, and they fall silent for the rest of the day.

Enkidu knows he is just a man. He didn't ask for these adventures. He is only his father's son, whatever size or strength he might possess. And now he is a killer. What story can he tell to make sense of that?

These young men were his people. They still are, as much as that is possible now. But he isn't a young boy anymore, running at one of their meetings in some loud unconscious pack.

Enkidu looks at Domun and Haladasi. He sees a shadow of himself before his adventures started happening. In days before, he would have simply fallen into their mind-sense and walked with them without thought. Shaping his feet to their path, at the brow of a hill or along a deer trail in the plains.

The land still gives him everything he needs.

He still remembers to give thanks.

Even so, he feels a distance.

He has words of the city language now, making meaning of what once had simply been itself.

His mind never fully quiets. He has even learned a word to name this sense of his own awareness, but that word makes little difference.

And there is another word, another new feeling. This longing for those times together, back when he was a boy.

But thoughts and longings and words notwithstanding, Enkidu is still a man. All those months past, he had been a stranger in those strange places. Now here he is body to body with his cousins. Days of walking and finding food and making camp.

They wrestle.

They wrestle like dancing. A joining of bodies, they don't fight for dominance, though they do learn about their strength and their weakness.

Holding on to each other, then twisting away, they let muscles speak their own language. Weight and balance and friction and momentum, impossible to misunderstand, they pull and lift and twist.

The bodies know what they know. Afterwards, they are tired and hungry and go looking for water and something to eat.

And then one day they killed a gazelle. They hadn't been following a herd. They are young men traveling unencumbered, and they could find enough food for a day, or decide to be hungry if that was what they felt. But one day as they were out walking, they find the tracks of a small band of gazelle, so of course they turned to follow.

Only three men is probably not enough to succeed at hunting gazelle, but they are young and why not try? Watching from a distance as the animals are grazing, they see a grown male born this year, at the outer edge of the herd, moving in a way that says young and incautious.

The herd sees the men. One, then two, then all the gazelle together lift their heads from the grass, swivel their ears, and watch the men watching them. But the men keep enough distance that the animals don't spook. The gazelle are wary, but they slowly bend back to their grazing.

The three men agree on their target. Enkidu and Haladasi stand and retrace their steps, letting the gazelle see them walking lazily away. When they have gone far enough, they turn and take a wide arc to either side of the herd, making three points of a circle around them.

Domun creeps up closer to the young buck, rises to a crouch, and lets off an arrow. He gets a shallow shot to the rump, and the herd startles and runs. The young buck jumps, looks confused, and runs straight toward Haladasi, so near that he can get a solid shot to the neck just in front of the shoulder.

The rest of the herd disappears over a rise, but the wounded buck can't keep up, and the three men spend the day following him until he wears out and they can finish him.

They thank the buck for getting close enough to their arrows. Then they get to work. Each of them has done this many times and it is companionable work. Cleaning the carcass, skinning and sectioning the body, building a rack of sticks, and setting the meat over a smoky fire to cure.

This is not the kind of work to be expected from three young men traveling loose through the landscape, but work done in company with brothers and sisters and parents and cousins. Camping in one place for more than just one or two days, using every part of the animal. Making sure that the job is done properly, tending the fire through the rainy night. This is the kind of work they would be doing if they were with their families right now.

They sing the gazelle songs together, and this makes them feel like brothers. But at the same time, they notice that three is a very small number to do the gazelle dances, hardly enough to make a whole family.

Now and then, as they tend to the meat and scrape the hide, they look out to the distance of the land around them. Their eyes trace the shapes where the hills meet the cloudy sky, and they tell each other stories about when they were young boys with their families.

Huddling close around a small fire, their backs to the chilly wind, picking the last meat off the bones of their gazelle as the rain clouds blow over, a body feels alive, no matter what words are spoken.

— 10 —

When the clouds clear, Enkidu looks at the blue of the sky and says the city words that describe it. He sees himself watching the sky. But that seeing doesn't make him feel such a stranger this time. Perhaps he is nearly ready to go find his family.

Domun has started talking about going back to his family, too. There is a certain young woman he says he might persuade to marry him. Haladasi says he could stay out on the trail for a while longer. Maybe afterwards, he will get some sheep and follow them wherever they go.

As he says this, Domun starts teasing him about being an outcast wandering around all alone, but then he remembers Enkidu and stops short.

Just then Haladasi looks up and asks a question. "When we go back to our families, you know that they will ask us about what we saw and what we did. Do we have any good stories to tell them? Of course, Enkidu has had many adventures to tell, but, you and me, Domun, do you think we have anything worth telling about the time we've been away?"

Domun says, "That's true, the women do like a good story, and we probably need to impress our young cousins as well. Do you remember that story my family told whenever they talked about young men going traveling? The one about my father's father and his two brothers who went to the western sea? Then only my grandfather came back to tell about it? After he came back, every-body wanted to hear him tell that story over and over."

Haladasi smiles, "I remember hearing that story, and I'd like to go to the sea. If we went, then we'd have a great story too, maybe something like the ones we keep asking Enkidu to tell us about his time in the city."

Domun wonders if it is too far, if they will ever get back to their homes. Enkidu says he wants to return to his family soon too. But he is with his brothers. If they decide to go to the western sea he is willing to go with them.

Haladasi jumps up and points toward the setting sun. "What if we walk due west, just like the stories say, and then see what we find? Maybe keep going until the new moon right before the win-ter solstice. And then if we don't get to the sea, we can tell every-one that it isn't really there."

Domun gets swept up in Haladasi's enthusiasm, and they decide to go. They stand side by side, arms hanging on each other's backs, feeling happy. Walking becomes straighter and simpler when you have a destination, everything makes more sense, and the ground pulls in only one direction.

For a month they have been walking, and they keep walking for another month. Or has it been three?

The rainy season keeps raining, but their time together has made them brothers. One of them will laugh at a joke that comes to him, and the others will laugh too just as he starts to tell it.

They move together as one loose body, not touching but con-nected. They come upon a skittish hyrax that has gotten a little too far from its burrow. Enkidu steps between the animal and its hole. Haladasi heads it off as it runs. And Domun moves around to chase it back to Enkidu. The three of them make the quick moves that the others expect, each taking their position without even a word.

And on a warm day when the sun finally comes out, they stand shoulder to shoulder and make a single six-legged shadow, feeling strong and still with the heat on their backs.

They know all of each other's stories now, so at night passing time by the fire, they might start in the middle and mix the parts around, laughing as they jump in and out of bodies and times. Then it feels like the story tells itself, one of the brothers speaking and then the next, saying things they didn't know that they knew.

Sometimes they tell the old legends of their people, looking up at the stars and telling the tales of the hunter and the serpent.

Sometimes they do without human words.

Enkidu hoots like an owl.

Domun starts slowly clapping his hands.

Haladasi joins, clacking with sticks.

Enkidu changes to singing like a wolf.

Their music goes out into the darkness where the night animals hear them. They laugh, calling back and forth to the owls and the jackals.

Domun still hasn't made sense of Enkidu's story. How could he leave his family and friends and set out all by himself? Or what Enkidu did when he was in Uruk, walking away from a woman like Shamhat?

Enkidu has tried to explain that it was not so simple. There were forces pulling in different directions. But his explanations don't seem to explain it. Lately, when Domun asks, Enkidu just smiles and gives him a shrug.

Domun is confused by how Enkidu experienced the richness of the city, and somehow this didn't soothe his sadness, only increased it. Enkidu's sadness makes sense to him in his own story. He has told them about his sadness for Ninsigal. About his sadness for what his people have lost, and the fattest and sweetest fruits taken by the kings and the cities.

He has told them about the way people live in the city. But how to explain what the people in the city have also lost? Their marrow is sucked out, and maybe they don't even know it. So Enkidu is left to carry their sadness too.

But it is such a long walk from this calm little campfire all the way back to Uruk, and the people there in the city coming and going and doing their business. Maybe the feeling can't be explained, it can only be felt.

Haladasi doesn't speak much, only when the words well up. Enkidu often finds himself feeling content just standing beside him, listening to the wind and watching the horizon. They keep walking westward and the hills become mountains and they struggle to keep warm. There wasn't anyone to tell them that they were silly to go to the sea during winter.

But one day they come to the last ridge, now the land slopes downward in front of them, only lower hills beyond. The rain has stopped for a little while and there is a fresh breeze clearing the clouds. The wind smells different from anything they remember. Like air near the river but without the reeds and the mud.

They set their camp on a flat spot just down from the ridge. They sit together watching the sky and the green of the hills below them. Just as the sun touches the horizon, they all slap each other and shout. "Did you see that? Doesn't that look like water below the sun? We've made it to the sea! Only a couple more days!"

Nearing the coast, they see more people. When they crest a hill they can see seaport towns in the distance. They pass small mud-brick villages where women are weaving in the courtyards, twining hemp for rope and sewing sails of woolen fabric. Men are pruning orchards, and women tending gardens. Large piles of baskets lean against walls of houses along the edge of a reedy marsh. In the grassy places, young men are grazing sheep. Here and there, groups of a few huts made of driftwood, covered with heavy cloth, a cow in the yard. At the seacoast they see people fishing for food and mending nets.

They have arrived at a sandy beach, and stand watching waves lap the shore. It is a whole new world where land turns to water, and the water stretches as far as they can see.

They run into the water and splash and laugh like little boys. Dive, and all at once feel how cold the water is.

The water is salty! They run back up the beach and shiver, hold each other tight, and bounce up and down trying to get warm.

There are other people on the shore, and the brothers approach them, cobbling together some language and gestures, they ask if they may camp here.

The people say, "Yes, of course."

Their new neighbors are friendly, asking them questions in language that they almost understand. Trying to explain where they've come from, Domun points to the inland ridge, and makes a motion for "far." Then they all go to the tide pools and catch some crabs that they roast with seaweed over a small driftwood fire.

In the morning, the brothers go for a long walk southward down the beach. They climb around a rocky point jutting out into the water, and in the next cove, they come upon a man working on a large wooden boat that lies tilted over on the sand.

The man waves his hand in greeting and when they get near, he wipes the sweat from his brow with a large hairy forearm which he rubs onto the side of his worn woolen skirt. After they do their greetings, he tells them how he was sailing and a storm hit. It ripped his sails, threw his boat up onto the beach, and broke his rudder. His three crewmen walked back home to their families while he did repairs, but now he has finished and there is nobody to help him get the boat off the beach so he can go back to fishing.

The three brothers are happy to help. Domun and Haladasi heave on a pair of ropes tied to the stern while Enkidu sets his feet in the sand and shoves on the bow. The fisherman digs sand out of the way and uses a long pole to lever the boat up when it gets stuck. They drag the boat into the water until a wave lifts and floats it and they give another shove and climb aboard.

The fisherman hands them oars to push against the bottom, he makes hand motions for turning the bow seaward and moving out to get more depth.

They are in deeper water and the boat pitches in the swell, the fisherman hands the tiller to Haladasi, and he puts ropes in Domun's and Enkidu's hands and they heave on the ropes to set the sail.

They head westward and the swell is bigger now and the land behind them is just a thin pitching strip that comes and goes out of sight. They have never had the land move around like that before, and each of them gets sick one after the other. But with the wind on their faces and their stomachs emptied, it turns out that being in a boat on the water is really fun if they are careful to keep an eye on the horizon.

The man shows them nets and tackle and how to throw the nets and retrieve them and they are pretty clumsy at it, but it's not really complicated, and after a while, they have caught many baskets of fish. Now they must hurry to shore before the fish start to stink.

The fisherman drives the boat onto the sand and shouts his arrival. Soon his wife comes down the beach with an armload of baskets and a baby slung to her chest. The wind blows her thin shawl from her hair. Two young girls and a boy run ahead of her to meet him, happy and yelling, and they unload the fish as a crowd gathers and there is plenty for all of them.

The fisherman gives the three brothers a whole basket of fish and Enkidu and Haladasi carry it between them, back to their little camp, where they make a fire and roast the fish and have a great feast, sharing their bounty with the people they met the day before, and with some other people who come to join them.

Domun sees a woman passing by with her unmarried daughter, and he calls out and runs to give the woman a roasted fish. Domun and the daughter use hand signs, attempting to introduce themselves. The woman bows her thanks for the fish, weathered hands pressed together. The daughter smooths her linen tunic, a smile on her tanned face.

Haladasi wants to go back fishing tomorrow, the fisherman has told them that they were good workers and any time they want to go out with him they are welcome. The three brothers agree to keep fishing for a few more days. It isn't long before they have gotten the rhythm of sailing the boat, pulling together on the ropes and the nets.

And so they keep sailing and fishing until the new moon after the winter solstice.

Haladasi is a true fisherman now, he says the rolling sea is just like tall grass blowing in waves, but sailing a boat is so much faster than walking. Domun isn't a fisherman at heart, but he keeps on fishing and he is handy at splicing ropes and repairing the nets. He has found the young woman's house and brings more fish. Her mother wipes her hands on her apron and invites Domun to join them for their meal of barley, fish, and vegetables.

Domun meets the rest of her family, and they have started learning some of each other's language. Now he spends most of his nights camped behind their house with the young woman's brothers and cousins.

Enkidu is glad to see that his brothers have found places for themselves, it is time for him to go find his father. They have one last bonfire and feast with all their new friends, everyone hugging Enkidu and begging him not to go.

Weren't all of them just like a big family during the solstice celebration? Does Enkidu really want to go back to traveling alone? What will they do without him to translate their jokes for Domun and Haladasi?

All of them eat a little too much and they lean against each other around the fire, singing a song whose words repeat in a round, something about:

> *There's a boat in the moon*
> *And a goat eating stars*
> *You're leaving too soon*
> *And going too far...*

In the morning Enkidu hugs his brothers. He thanks them for sharing their stories. And for helping him re-learn how to walk. Then he turns his back to the sea and walks east on the path to find his father and brother.

— II —

Enkidu climbs inland over the ridge, down into the valley then up the next ridge, finding the direction to look for his family.

Nearly every year during the second new moon after the winter solstice, they camp at the old village site in the basin south of the basalt desert. Walking eastward with his bag of parched fish, the saltbush on the hills and the tamarisks in the creeks are starting to look familiar. He walks quickly, he doesn't need to hunt for food.

Using his movement across the land to quiet his thoughts. He knows his family loves him, but he worries that when he returns, they will end up carrying too much of his trouble.

After days of this, Enkidu begins to see basalt rocks showing dark and red-grey in the pale sandy soil. They lead him to the usual place where his family camps. Coming over a rise, he finds their camp just as he hoped. He can see his nephew in front of their tent and shouts out his greeting. His nephew yells in return and dives into the tent, and then everyone comes out and runs to greet him, the women ululating and the men hooting and his nephew jumping up and down. His sister runs up and grabs him around the neck, and he has to carry her back to their camp.

They celebrate his homecoming as if it were the birth of a new child. His mother's brother's wife and his father's brother's wife and his brother's wife's voices echo against the rocky hills.

Everyone is shouting, "Enkidu is back! We heard you were alive, but we didn't know where you were! We heard you were going to the cedar forest, is that really true? Where else have you been? Tell us everything you have done and seen!"

Enkidu shivers. He will tell them everything.

His nephew is so much bigger, and he's excited about this large man, his uncle, but it's hard to know how much he remembers. Enkidu tells his story to his family. How he has been a fisherman and guide to a king and went to Uruk and lived in the temple.

The story takes two days to tell, and then there are more questions and Enkidu has to tell the story from a different direction. He watches the faces of his family members as they react to his tale. He is happy when they laugh, but the bad parts are bad. He doesn't want his family to feel worse about those parts than he does. Everyone is quieter after he tells about the three soldiers.

Part way through the next telling he stops. "Did anyone ever learn anything about Ninsigal?"

They all shake their heads, "No." Enkidu tells them that he hasn't learned much either. He describes some of the rich men he met. He tells them what he knows of the soldiers and some of the rumors he heard about them. But he doesn't know anything for certain.

Except for the men that he killed.

"Still, I have a feeling that Ninsigal is alive somewhere."

His family crowds up against Enkidu.

They sing the mourning songs swaying by the fire, grieving for the part of him that died with those men. How could it be that their son came onto such a path?

There are ways to heal a condition like his, but they all take a long time.

After a few days, they break camp and begin walking southeast in the direction of the pass where they can cross the ridge to a trail going northward, toward the big spring equinox festival.

Late one night, Enkidu wakes with a start. He sees the moon above the western horizon, a little younger than half. His dream woke him and it lingers in his eyes.

It was the large black bird. He recognized the bird from the dream when Ninsigal was carried away, the dream before he heard of her kidnapping.

The bird is flying high in the air, much as it did when it took Ninsigal away. But now the bird is coming toward him.

The bird is alone, he doesn't see Ninsigal. It circles lower, looming large, its shadow passes over him. The bird lands a few paces from Enkidu and turns her dark eye toward him.

Black feathers have weathered to brown, many of them tattered at their ends. The bird has a wound in her breast, she is bleeding, giving off heat and a sense of sadness.

Enkidu speaks to the bird, "Wait, I will bring some water. Let me tend your wound."

The bird turns her head away and closes her eyes, settling her body to the ground. She tucks her feet under and folds her wings along her back. Her head nods as if going to sleep, then falls limp to the ground, her wings slipping loose at her sides.

The bird is dead.

⁂

Wide awake now, Enkidu lies watching the sky for the rest of the night. After a while, the stars slowly dim on the eastern horizon. The pale blue of predawn rises to hide them, turning pale, then yellow pushing the blue up overhead.

He goes out walking in the cool light before sun breaks the horizon, making a circle around their camp. Checking the tracks and scat for news of last night's animals. He listens for faint rustling in the bushes, the peeping first notes of the new morning's bird songs.

His dream weighs on him. He makes no effort to interpret it. He knows it is bad. Instead, he spends his days walking with his family and foraging for food along the trail. He sits beside the campfire and he lays down to sleep. All the while there is a weight pulling against his breath.

Muscles expand his chest to bring air into his lungs, and all the sky is connected. With every in-breath, he has to pull the whole of it. This is heavy work, moving all the air in the sky. Enkidu is never not aware of it. A continuous effort, even after an evening meal when he is sitting at camp, or laying down ready to sleep.

But this is his labor, and he does it willingly. At least it is something he can do. True that it is heavy, all the air in the sky.

But look up, see how blue it is!

Then a swell and blush and fade of colors. Day changes to night and then it changes back. He carries the burden of his dream, knowing without really knowing. This lump of grief that has come to him. It is his, and he carries it.

He even takes some solace from the ache in his chest. It is not a sharp pain to make him wince, it is thick, it has texture, and he can feel it moving. Like hot desert sand somehow surrounding and pressing against him.

The pain reminds him that he is alive.

Traveling is different now, carrying the weight of the sky. He is glad to be with his family. Of course, they have noticed that he is in pain. All he knows to say is that he is sad for Ninsigal. His father and his brother put their arms around him, and that helps him hold the weight.

Then another family joins their path and they camp together. They are a sister and a brother and their families, cousins of cousins of Enkidu's father.

They have news of Ninsigal.

This family has been traveling west and north since the last full moon. It was then they found Ninsigal's body. There was a small place hidden by a group of boulders. She'd been dead for a few days, partly eaten by scavengers, but they could still see some likeness, and there were remains of her clothing that helped them identify her.

And a curious thing, there was a bronze knife lying beside her. It was finely made, with a carved ivory handle. They buried Ninsigal's remains there among the rocks, and they sang the songs of grieving for her.

The families mourn Ninsigal together, wailing by the fire. They sing the songs again. Each of them feels her death differently. The grief songs bring those different parts together and make a larger whole.

Enkidu catches his breath and lifts up his hands. He lets his breath out and the wailing subsides. Another breath, and he begins telling the dream he'd had, about the large black bird.

Everyone is silent until Enkidu has finished his telling.

His father and brother put their arms over his shoulders, hum a low dirge, and sway, and all the rest of the party joins in, and they keep going until everyone is exhausted. Then they all hug each other and turn to go to sleep.

— 12 —

In the morning they pick themselves up and make the morning meal. Enkidu is awake this morning, the sun caught his eye right at dawn. He is filled with questions for his father's cousin's cousin.

"What kind of clues did you find, how did she die?"

"Could you tell what direction she came from before she got to that place?"

"What about that bronze knife? Where is it now?"

His cousin answers, "The knife? It had too much power, nobody would touch it. Your cousin dug another hole beside Ninsigal's grave, he pushed the knife into the hole with a stick, then covered it with dirt."

So Enkidu asks them, "Please tell me how to find the place where Ninsigal is buried. I need to go there right away."

His father's cousin's cousin tells him the way, it is simple, he needs only retrace the steps that brought them here. So that is what Enkidu will do. He hugs his father and brother and his brother's wife and his nephew and his father's brother's wife and all of his second cousins and wishes them good travels. He thanks his father's cousin's cousins for their news.

The news of Ninsigal is bad, but it is better than not knowing. He says he is sorry that he is in so much of a hurry. That he isn't able to stay and share more of his stories with them. He has been on such a long journey, he can't hold himself from going on with it. The weight that had been pressing his body to the ground is now at his back pushing him onward.

Enkidu's mother's brother's wife and his father's brother's wife hold his left and right arms. They can see that they won't be able to keep him from going.

"We were so happy when you came back to us, but now we worry that you are leaving too soon. Remember that you have only just started your return. Walking with those two young men was a good beginning, but it will take a lot more time before you are done. When you insisted upon staying all by yourself at the apricot thicket, we worried that there would be trouble. We are worried still."

Enkidu responds, "Yes, you are right, there was trouble. I know it is always dangerous to walk alone. I knew you were right even then at the apricot thicket. But whatever was holding me to stay, then pushing me to go was so strong that I couldn't do anything else. Just as it is now. I'll do this one more thing. Then I'll come back to you."

He hugs them all one more time, kisses his sister, and he is on his way, walking east and south toward a place in the hills nearly half the way to Uruk. His feet find the trail going back the way his father's cousin's cousins had come.

His mind rushes ahead of him, and he has to keep bringing it back. He trains his attention to the smells of damp soil and new growth along his path. There is a familiar acrid taste at the back of his tongue. He checks the sky for black birds.

Then, after days of walking, he arrives at the place enclosed by boulders. There are seven of them in a rough circle, large grainy sandstone as tall as a man, rounded and solidly rooted in place, with a gap between two of them large enough to allow a man to enter the circle.

The sandy soil inside the ring of boulders has a patch that is a darker color, siltier and looser than the rest. Enkidu's chest pounds, thump of blood in his ears, he steps slowly to one end of the body-length patch of disturbed ground. Pulse pressing at his temples, and heat in cheeks and forehead, his eyes get full.

He drops to his knees, his chest swells and tightens, the air feels harsh like smoke in his throat. Falling forward, arms outspread, cheek to dirt, the pressure leaks from his eyes and salt water drips across his face. Hardened trail dust in his nose flushed out by new liquid, mixing with tears, makes a spot of mud pasted to his face.

A catch in his stomach as he exhales, face in sandy mud, his nose tickles but the muscles to sneeze are doing something else. He feels the press of grit on his knees and the tops of his feet. A grain of sand on his tongue, he rolls it across the roof of his mouth, is this the last bit of Ninsigal?

The sand grain feels large like a pebble between his teeth. He crunches down and gets a scatter of grit in his mouth. Mineral, nothing like Ninsigal. He wipes his tongue across teeth, and raises his face from the ground to spit, more for the mud patch.

Exhaustion — his shoulders loosen. He closes his eyes and drops his face back to the ground.

Enkidu awakens with the heat of sun on his back.

He picks up his face from the dirt and rolls to a sitting position. His head feels warm and humid, strong smell of his scalp in the first waking breaths, almost like a haze of fog but warmer, animal.

He's had a dream. It had gotten light, and his eyes open. He is still lying on the ground. The boulders are gone and all around him is grassland. The ground beneath him starts heaving, pushing him up, Enkidu scrambles backward from the lifting bulge, away from the grave.

The surface cracks open and Ninsigal rises out. She is old, her skin is thick, folded, and grey, she stands on four legs, solid as tree stumps. She is a large grazing animal with a long heavy jaw and small eyes, comical ears swivel at the top of her head. She has a powerful horn pointing up from above her mouth and nostrils.

Enkidu is glad to see her, strange as she is. Ninsigal is lonely and says nothing, her eyes fix Enkidu with a look of sadness. So many years have passed and she is the last of her kind.

Then the hump of her shoulders is drawn upward, a stream pulling into the air, stretching in a ribbon and turning darker, her body reassembles into a large soaring bird.

Enkidu is a bird now, too. He and Ninsigal are flying together above rocky cliffs tufted with yellow grass. Beyond the cliffs is a horizon of water as far as he can see.

Enkidu is happy to be flying with Ninsigal, he feels his heart beating. Soaring, she shows no sign of effort. Feathers at her wingtips spread like fingers feeling the breeze. Her wings are as wide as the height of a man, her chest powerful and compact. She is a majestic bird and she smells of death.

Together, above and below, they fly a great distance, the landscape beneath them changing, now wetter and wooded.

Enkidu smiles, it's fun to be a bird. Ninsigal bends her wings and dives toward the forest below them. Enkidu follows her more slowly, still learning his wings. He lands on a sandy beach at the bend of a shallow sunlit river.

Looking around, he finds Ninsigal, she is now a large tree growing on the riverbank in front of him. He is a man now, he sees his hands and feet. Tree Ninsigal is taller than any tree he's ever seen, she is surrounded by her sisters who are nearly as tall as she is, the lowest of their massive branches many times his height above him.

He hears a low-pitched hum, deep and dirge-like, it is coming from Ninsigal and her tree family. Is she trying to speak to him? If this is her language, he doesn't understand it. He looks along the river where the forest meets the sandy riverbank, and notices that there are stumps where trees have been cut down.

The light turns bluish and the dirge hums more intense, it vibrates the air and Enkidu feels it in the ground, coming up through his feet, the sky is a blur of days and nights flying past.

He sees new tree sprouts pushing up out of the ground, six or eight of them from around each of the stumps, a wide circle centered on the place where the cut tree had been. The new trees grow fast in the strange humming light, tall, reaching up toward Ninsigal.

A splash in the river draws Enkidu's ear. He turns and looks behind him, sees the water, and remembers that he is thirsty. He kneels down and bends to the river, but before he can drink, the water ruins his thirst. The river is cloudy brown, there are darker flecks floating, the water smells like something has died.

He turns back to Ninsigal but now the forest is gone, more time has passed and the sandy beach is turned to gravel, overgrown with vine-choked scrubby brush where the forest had been.

Smell of dust, hot leaves, and tar, then Enkidu is back at the boulders where he started, now hovering above them. He'd hoped to see Ninsigal again, whatever her form, but now he is alone. He sees far away, and tiny details up close, both at the same time. In the distance are cities and people living in them, all busy going here and there.

He hears their footsteps, each one distinctly and all of them together — combined, they make a low roar. Nearby below him, he sees the boulders lit by the sun. With each footstep in the city, he sees a small grain of sand detach from a boulder and trickle to the ground.

He awakes from the dream tired, with sweat at the back of his neck.

Enkidu lifts himself up and backs away from Ninsigal's grave. He looks at the boulders and they are quiet, not moving. They've seen everything before, and this latest misfortune doesn't distress them. This is a good place for Ninsigal, and Enkidu takes some consolation from that. But he still feels something unsettled.

His eye is drawn to a small patch of disturbed ground with a flat rock set on it. He gets up and steps outside the rock nest, looking around until he sees an old sage bush growing from a rocky place at the edge of the surrounding grass. He faces the bush, nods to it, then kneels and pulls off a rough branch from low on the trunk.

He sits on the ground with his back to one of the boulders, and pinning down the edge of his skirt with the broken end of the sage branch, he rips his skirt with a sharp tug and tears off a piece. Then he strips the sage stick, puts the leaves on the sheepskin scrap, and sets the twigs in a little pile on the dirt.

He stands and stretches his back, then takes a couple of steps to a clump of tall grass. He kneels in front of it, nods to the grass clump, and one by one he pulls out stems until he has a fat handful. Sitting back against one of the boulders, feeling the light morning breeze and the sun on his shoulders, he braids a cord, plaiting together the grass stems. It calms him to work with his hands. The dream lingers just outside his vision.

Then he wraps the sage leaves into the sheepskin and stands, takes the stick and braided cord and sheepskin back inside the boulders. He kneels in front of the flat rock that sits on the patch of disturbed soil, and takes a deep breath. The rock was put here recently, it will move without trouble. He takes the stick and pushes the rock to his right. Pause and a breath before he takes the stick and digs the loose soil out to the left. There in the hole he finds the knife.

He sees how it fits exactly into this bed of fresh soil, and it must not stay here. He opens the sheepskin sage bundle at the edge of the hole, then pries the knife out, awkward using the stick, tumbling it onto the sage leaves. Dirt still clings to the knife, but he can see it was well made, sharp with a curving bronze blade and round ivory handle.

There are markings and figures scribed into the ivory — the artisan rubbed blacking into the marks to make them stand out. Many hands have held this knife, making it, admiring it, carrying it, putting it to use. The grain of the ivory tells of the animal it was taken from.

Enkidu shivers. Beneath the dirt on the blade is a crust of red-brown residue. He closes the sheepskin tight around the knife and ties it shut with the grass cord. Leaving the bundle on the ground, he stands and backs away to the other side of the rock nest. He has made a package of the death knife. This must mean that he is to take it away from here.

He leans against the boulder behind him, feeling its rough surface and the last of its morning coolness on his back. He looks at the bundle, and the sandy ground, and the shadow of the boulder across from him. He crosses back to the knife hole, pushes the loose dirt back in, and moves the flat rock back on top where it was.

Enkidu knows that this knife must be taken away from here, away from his homeland, away from Ninsigal's remains. He can feel the power of the knife, it is the power of the city.

He remembers Shamhat telling him of the people competing to rule the temple. The men who hold power over the temple of the city. Clearly, this knife belongs to those men.

How did Ninsigal come to be here with this thing from the men of the city? Are they the same men Shamhat was asking for his help to fight? He needs to go back to Uruk and find her.

Tying a long loop in the grass cord that holds the bundle, he lifts it over his head and shoulders and carries it slung behind his back. He doesn't want to look at it, but he can feel the knife in the bundle behind him, bumping his back as he walks, propelling him toward the city.

— 13 —

In the evening after their final day at the logging camp, Gilgamesh cheers his company. The ax men brag about the trees they have cut. They've made notches in their ax handles for each one they felled, and now they are comparing, seeing who has the most.

To spread the glory, Gilgamesh holds up the hand of the chief cook. "Here is my champion cook! He makes the best roast donkey anywhere." And then he holds up the hand of the captain of the drovers. "And he drives the best roasting donkeys!"

The cooks dump all the remaining barley flour in a large bowl and bake piles of flat breads. Everyone is feeling festive and they drink down the last of the beer. It is after the fall equinox, and the moon a little more than first quarter. Everyone is happy to be heading for home before the rainy season starts.

The next morning they pile their tools and their weapons and their remaining supplies onto the four large log rafts. Teams of men slosh into the river and heave the rafts off the shallow mud bank, then climb aboard and pole the rafts out into the main current of the river.

Behind them, they leave two hillsides denuded of trees. Stumps and piles of slashed branches, trampled undergrowth wilting, newly exposed to the sun.

The men lounge on the rafts, tired and happy, ready for a lazy trip home. As they were loading the rafts, Gilgamesh scanned the camp for Enkidu. Now he watches the riverbank slowly drift past, there's been no sign of the wild man. He probably wandered off to the hills — not much of a surprise.

But the campaign is a great success, his men are happy, and they laugh together like men who have done heavy work as a team. Besides, on the river, they don't need the wild man. Gilgamesh can wait until they get home to decide how to punish Enkidu for leaving him.

Lookouts above the river see Gilgamesh and his crew floating downstream with stolen timber, and they run to send word to Zialu, king of Ebla. Zialu is furious — this is not the first of his arguments with Gilgamesh, there have been a number of them, and this is one too many.

The king instructs his ministers to prepare an army to go to Uruk. Meanwhile, he gathers forty of his soldiers and they chase Gilgamesh down the river. It is the end of the dry season, and it is not difficult for a soldier to outrun a raft on the sluggish river.

Zialu catches up with Gilgamesh just above Mari. The bowmen of Ebla whoop a war cry and shoot arrows low over the heads of the men on Gilgamesh's rafts. Zialu shouts to bring the flotilla of rafts to the bank, or else they will all be killed like ducks stuck in mud. Even Gilgamesh can see that Zialu isn't joking.

The rafts are slow and heavy, and the men push on poles and jump off the rafts with ropes, digging their feet into the river mud to drag the rafts to the shallow eddies. Zialu's men follow down the river with arrows ready so Gilgamesh won't change his mind.

Gilgamesh swaggers up the bank with a dozen soldiers to talk with the king of Ebla. "Hey Zialu, my friend, what can I do for you today?"

Zialu is a thin man, his beard flecked with grey. Gilgamesh stands head and shoulders taller, but Zialu's lieutenants move in close to make up the difference. Zialu just glares at Gilgamesh and tells his captain to go count the logs and make an estimate of their length. The captain comes back and quotes a value in gold for the logs.

Gilgamesh knows he will end up having to pay for the stolen timber. And now he knows its value.

Zialu has enough soldiers here to win a fight if it came to that, but they all know that fighting would be a useless waste of some of their best men. Gilgamesh calculates that he can drive a tilted bargain, it will cost him less to keep the cedar logs because Zialu wants to avoid a pitched battle. Though it would have been more fun to get away with stealing.

They stand in the sun on the riverbank arguing about what Gilgamesh must pay Zialu, and when they finish they clasp hands to swear an oath. Then the men heave the rafts back into the current downriver to Uruk.

Gilgamesh shouts to Zialu, "Give my regards to the queen!"

When they finally get within sight of Uruk, teams of men pick up ropes, jump off the rafts, and wade to the riverbank. It is a couple of days past the winter solstice, more than four months since they first left Uruk. The river was lazy at the end of the dry season when they set off from the cedar forest, but now the rains have started in earnest. The men dig in their heels and heave at the barges, teaming up to pull against the rising current. They trail the rafts down the riverbank, heaving again to bring the rafts closer in, then to the city pier where they loop the ropes around the pilings, tying them off. Anyone who wants to use the pier now will need to clamber across the log rafts.

Gilgamesh climbs onto Uruk pier. He lifts his fists in the air and shouts triumph. The rafts and the noise are drawing a crowd. Two of his men carry the auroch bull head and parade it behind him, while Gilgamesh strides up the pier toward the city gate. The ax men follow with blades held high, they have polished the axes so they shine in the cloudy light, and everybody falls in for a victory procession.

They march to the center of the city, and the parade loops around itself on the temple plaza, then swirls in confusion where its head meets its tail. Gilgamesh climbs the steps above the plaza, orders the temple beer jars brought out, and leads the crowd in cheering.

After the crowd has turned its attention to beer, Gilgamesh troops back to the palace, followed by a gaggle of rich men looking for favors. He orders the cooks to keep the palace banquet table filled, and a continuous supply of beer. He moves among the rich men, laughing and telling his adventures. He watches their faces as they flatter him, looking to see who will make a useful ally. The palace courtesans mingle in the crowd looking to pick up loose favors.

One of Gilgamesh's ministers follows him, keeping a tally of the king's gifts of timber, which of the rich men has just been made richer, and what has been promised in return. The traders and craftsmen swear allegiance to Gilgamesh and promise that their work will sing the glory of their hero-king.

A pair of messengers run back and forth to the temple scribes dictating the details to be recorded. As the evening wears on, everyone gets drunker, and the scribes have left their tables for the night, but all the hopeful traders keep making promises, whether or not they can keep them or even remember them.

The next day, Gilgamesh has his first minister go with two soldiers to visit Ma-tur, his young sister, to inform her that she will be partial payment for the timber theft and that she now belongs to

Zialu, so she'd better get busy packing her things. He tells his trea-
surer to find that lump of lapis lazuli weighing one hundred minas,
the one he swindled off those traders from Indus.

The cooks work day and night to keep the banquet table filled.
The serving girls have given up trying to keep the dining hall clean,
they just push the debris into a corner. The party at the palace
keeps on going, Gilgamesh has never been more popular.

Gilgamesh has been back in Uruk for more than a month before
he wakes up one morning and the palace is mostly quiet, an old
moon fading in the west. The cedar forest campaign was a perfect
adventure, there is only one more detail he has to take care of.

— 14 —

Gilgamesh puts on his formal purple tunic and fits a gold band
on his head. His first minister arrives at Gilgamesh's rooms wearing
his court costume, carrying his gift. They walk together to the
temple of Inanna. They are met by the priestess of the day at her
reception room, and the first minister bows and makes a request
that she grant Gilgamesh an audience with Shamhat, Lady of the
temple. The priestess nods at a eunuch, and Gilgamesh and his
minister wait. Soon, the eunuch returns with two others.

Gilgamesh must leave his weapons outside, and the first minister
will not be coming with them. The first eunuch inspects the gift
that Gilgamesh has brought for the Lady, then hands it back to
him. He may bring it to her.

The eunuchs collect Gilgamesh's dagger and escort the first minister outside. Two of the three eunuchs return and lead Gilgamesh
down a short corridor to a reception room. There are two chairs
on either side of a table set with plates of leavened spelt breads
and dates. The first eunuch nods at a chair for Gilgamesh, who
stands beside it waiting for Shamhat.

She enters, dressed in her formal yellow robe and shawl, wearing closed slippers on her feet. Gilgamesh moves forward as if to kiss her in greeting, but a eunuch takes a step to block the way, and Shamhat slips into her place behind the chair across the table. She speaks her greeting, welcoming him to the temple of Inanna. Gilgamesh bows to her, puts on a little smile, and thanks her for accepting his visit.

Shamhat answers "Well, it is a special occasion when the king comes to Inanna. I hope that this visit proves to be worthy of your time."

Gilgamesh turns his hand palm up above the table, "Just to see you, Lady of Inanna, here in person is worthy enough. But I have also brought a gift for you."

Gilgamesh leans across the table and holds the gift parcel toward her. The nearest eunuch reaches in, lifts the packet from Gilgamesh's hand, and brings it around the table to Shamhat, opening it for her to see. She touches the contents and catches her breath.

Gilgamesh says, "My traders tell me that this scarf comes from a land far to the east where the people have learned to weave spiderwebs into cloth."

"Thank you, this is very beautiful." Shamhat smooths the fabric between her thumb and fingers. "I have never seen fabric so fine. I will be sure to show this lovely scarf to the women in our weaving workshop. And I would be grateful if next time you see your trader you could send him to see me, I'm curious to know more about this fabric and those weavers who made it. Would you like to sit down for a little refreshment? I'm certain that I haven't heard all the news of your campaign to the cedar forest."

Gilgamesh nods. The Lady sits down, and he follows. A eunuch offers Gilgamesh the plate of dates while another sets down a cup of beer for each of them. Gilgamesh smiles, chin forward, "Yes, we had an excellent trip to the forest. All of my men performed their duties admirably, and we brought home great new wealth for the people of Uruk. Of course, great wealth for Uruk must also benefit the temples. I would be honored if you would come and select the timbers that can be of use to your builders."

Shamhat brings her hands together in front of her, "That is very generous, and I appreciate the offer, thank you. However, timber is not part of my expertise, nor my responsibility here at the temple. I will happily tell our chief builder to meet with your men directly, and then send for your approval."

Gilgamesh nods, his smile slips a little sideways, "Oh yes, of course. You have charmed me such that I forget myself. Perhaps you would accompany your builder, and we could all go to the pier together. Something like a little picnic, don't you think?"

Shamhat takes a sip of beer and leans back in her chair. A small smile crosses her face. "Yes, that is a charming picture, to go on a little outing." She pauses a moment as if to see it, "But I'm certain that I would only get in the way, and my duties here at the temple really do fill my whole day. I regret that we will have to remain sat-isfied with only the idea of a picnic, rather than trying to make it actually happen."

Gilgamesh sits a little straighter in his chair but doesn't lose his smile. "Well, I insist that we find another way to meet again. Per-haps an evening meal at the palace? My personal cook has been doing some remarkable things lately."

Shamhat loses her smile. She gives a look to one of the eunuchs and he disappears out through the doorway. "You are requesting my company, rather than trying to take me by force? Is this a new way with you? Could this have anything to do with the time you spent in company with the wild man?"

Gilgamesh drops his smile, then starts to speak, but stops short.

After a moment he says, "I'm sorry that you feel that way. I don't know what I said to cause offense, but I'd like you to consider how important it is to the city that the temple cooperates with the king."

The eunuch comes back into the room followed by three others. They line up behind Gilgamesh.

Shamhat looks directly into Gilgamesh's eyes. "Yes, you are quite correct in principle, but you have spoken backward. Our temple historians tell us of times past, many years in duration, when the temple served the city, long before anyone called themselves king. Do you really believe that you would continue to be king if the temple didn't cooperate? For your part, it seems much more to the point that the king cooperates with the temple. Thank you for the visit, it was quite informative. My assistants will show you out."

Gilgamesh glares at her. With both hands on the table, he slowly slides back his chair. The hands curl to fists, and he raises himself up to full height, all the while keeping his eyes locked on Shamhat's.

She remains in her chair, radiating calm, her hands folded on the table, holding any danger response from showing on her face.

Gilgamesh breaks his stare, turns, and walks slowly out the doorway with straight, measured steps, down the corridor and out of the temple, with elbows held wide, never giving any notice to the five big eunuchs who follow him out.

Gilgamesh is enraged by the setback. Who is this chief prostitute, acting so haughty in front of him? He is Gilgamesh the king. Gilgamesh finds his first minister outside the temple and starts recounting the meeting with Shamhat, his face turning red from the effort of restraining his anger just so he can finish a sentence. Until he falls to simply shouting curses at her, stringing one after the other. Maybe it's time for Gilgamesh to finish the problem of that harlot Shamhat.

He knows Shamhat cannot speak officially for the temple of Inanna. He has heard of the power struggle in the temple, even if he hasn't kept up with all the details. He knows that his mother Ninsun has removed Lilitu as chief priestess and anointed herself. Already Ninsun has taken measures to make the temple more agreeable.

The temple produces and stores and distributes many valuable items. All the commerce of any importance to the city is overseen by the priesthood, and there are many people with a hand in the movement of this wealth both inside and outside of the temple.

Ninsun has made it her business to learn who those people are, and how they feel about the king. Now that she holds authority at Inanna, she has sent many of the temple officials away, to be replaced with her more reliable friends. Dealing with the eunuchs is more complicated, but she is making some progress in that regard, too.

Ninsun has declared that when citizens come to the temple to collect their ration of grain they are now required to swear that they live at Uruk, and before they enter the temple they must recite a brief oath praising the king. She has put her allies in charge of the distribution of Inanna's meals, and now Ninsun's friends are given the choicest portions of meat and the candied dates, leaving lesser-value mutton and flat breads for the working women and orphans.

She has installed her close friends as managers of the temple workshops, and they are now allowed to take personal payment for jobs done by the temple workers. One of the workshops has been converted to sharpening the spear points and swords that are made in a foundry run by one of Gilgamesh's friends.

As Gilgamesh walks back to the palace with his first minister, he goes on raging about Shamhat. When he finally drops himself onto his throne chair, Gilgamesh points to the door and orders the minister to remove Shamhat from Inanna and bring her to him.

The minister returns to the temple and meets with Ninsun. She frowns, ruining the effect of her carefully plaited hair and powdered cheeks. She lifts her chin to the minister and clasps her hands in front of her, flexing her biceps.

"Yes," she tells him, "you are quite correct that this kind of insolence toward the king has no place in our temple. I will have members of the temple guard collect this person and have her brought to the palace. I'm sorry for the inconvenience this has caused you, and I will take steps to ensure that it doesn't happen again."

Ninsun gives the word to her closest eunuchs, but when they approach Shamhat's chamber, they are met by other eunuchs who put hands on their chests and push them back the way they came, and both sides call for more help, and more eunuchs come running and pandemonium breaks out in the temple, wrestling eunuchs fill the hallways, ambushing around corners and chasing down the corridors, they fight each other to a draw.

Ninsun had counted on the eunuchs to be loyal to her, but they are not loyal to her person so much as to whoever holds power at the temple, whereas the eunuchs loyal to Shamhat are devoted to her personally.

Facing each other in a corridor, the two groups of eunuchs stare each other down. The senior member of Shamhat's loyalists raises a hand and speaks, "This is the temple of Inanna, we are all here for her glory and worship. What are we doing fighting each other over some squabble between mortals? Even those of you who are playing at the politics of the city must remember that the temple cannot operate without us. No king or priest can force us to do what we choose not to do. Let them play their small games without our help."

While the eunuchs at the center are working this out, farther back in the crowd, a few of Shamhat's partisans catch each other's eyes.

They slip out to find the first minister waiting in front of the temple. There are two soldiers guarding the minister, and the eunuchs come from behind and grab each of them around the middle and lift them off the ground, pinning their arms to their sides, holding them out of the way while one of their fellows lightly beat the minister, then together they shove the minister and soldiers out of the temple.

Word of the debacle reaches Gilgamesh, and he is furious.

He sends a squad of soldiers to force their way into the temple of Inanna and grab Shamhat. But she has already escaped to Anu with some of her loyal eunuchs.

— 15 —

The first minister picks himself up from the dust of the temple plaza. He sends the soldiers back to the palace with a message for Gilgamesh that he will meet with him tomorrow. He has no more patience today for Gilgamesh's demands. He has also bruised his hip and he doesn't want the soldiers to see him limping.

He watches the soldiers leave, smoothing his grey hair and beard before he starts the walk to his house. He tells himself that he isn't limping too badly, it's only a bruise. He holds himself upright, making an effort to walk with the dignity of his rank — even though the side of his tunic and skirt are pasted with grime. His leg isn't bending properly and the front of his sandal scrapes the ground, collecting dirt under his toes.

Surely many of the people coming and going in the plaza know who he is, he'd served as minister to the king even before Gilgamesh. He sets his gaze beyond the commoners, but still, he sees them watching him. He sees them look his way, then lean in to whisper to their friends. They shake their heads, he's certain he sees a look of pity. He is becoming steadily more furious.

The minister steps into his house and pushes the door closed behind him. He calls his personal servant to come take off his soiled clothing and prepare a bath. Then sends him away, telling him to fetch the guard to bring the slave girl.

The cook brings in the evening meal of braised lamb with flat bread and beer, setting it beside the bath. The hot water of the bath stings the minister's bruises at first, then the heat just turns his anger sullen. He ignores the cook's food and finishes the deep cup of beer.

The minister is out of the bath drying himself when the guard arrives at his chamber with the slave girl. The guard pulls off the girl's dress and drops it on the floor, making sure to not let his eyes fall on the minister. The guard dumps her on the bed and ties her wrists and ankles to the bed frame, then posts himself outside the door.

The first minister climbs onto the bed and rapes the slave girl like usual. "See," he tells himself, "I'm not old and worn out yet."

When he is finished he is exhausted, slumps to the side, and drifts off to sleep. The side of the minister's face is pressed to the bed, he is not moving except for his ribs lifting with his breath.

Ninsigal tests the cords on her wrists. She discovers that the guard has gotten careless and left some slack in the knot tying her left hand. A little slipping twist and bending the hand double, she picks the knot loose on that wrist, freeing it, then reaches over to the other.

She works slowly with small movements to not wake the man, and when his breathing sounds of solid sleep she rolls from under his arm. He snuffles and shifts and doesn't wake.

She sits up to untie her ankles, swings off the bed, and turns to find her dress on the floor, slips it over her head, and pads to the door. Carefully cracking it open, she sees that the guard has fallen asleep too, leaning against the wall beside the doorway, propping himself up with his spear.

Hanging from the guard's belt Ninsigal notices a bronze knife. She looks over her shoulder to the minister still sleeping, then with a slow smooth movement lifts the knife free. Easing back into the room, she quietly pushes the door shut, steps over to the bed, and slits the minister's throat, swift and straight, just like killing a goat.

She pushes a pillow onto his head until there is no more movement, then crosses the room, lightly opens the door, and skims out past the unconscious guard, her bare feet noiseless on the clay tile floor, the knife still in her hand.

Down the corridor, she pauses at every corner and doorway to take the scent and listen for anyone nearby. She finds a door out the back of the house, onto a narrow alley. There is no moon, and she doesn't know how many days it's been since she's seen the sky, but walking the slope of the city downhill will take her to the river, whichever direction. When she comes to a larger street, she takes a moment to look around and orient herself. High overhead she sees a part of the Hunter, not fully obscured by the clouds. She turns to the west, keeps walking, and soon in the dim star and cloud light she can see her way toward the wall of the city. She is approaching the western gate, walking on the moon shadow side of the street, even though there is no moon.

Piled bundles of marsh reeds beside a dark building make a narrow place where she can hide and wait until the gate opens at dawn.

In the morning, Ninsigal sees a group of women walking past her hiding place. They are going toward the city gates, carrying baskets and short-handled hoes. As they pass, she comes up behind them, blending into their group. She holds the knife flat against her wrist, her arm bent into a fold of her dress. The farm women give her a look, then glance back to their sisters and make no signs for the guards to see as they pass by.

Once clear of the gate and around a bend in the road, Ninsigal nods to the women, then makes quick for the reeds at the bank of the river.

She finds the shallows and fords across. Squatting in a blind of reeds on the far side of the river. Shivering from the cold water, she holds herself with arms around her knees until her dress has mostly dried and the sun is halfway to midday.

She edges out of the reeds onto a path, eyes down, keeping to the side. Judging her distance from other people and away from their dwellings so that she draws the least attention, no one takes time to notice whether she is coming or going.

She has gotten beyond the city people's places, and now the land is wilder. She feels the clench-ache in her jaw. How many days has that been?

She rubs the jaw muscles with the heel of her hand, wills them slightly looser. She stops and stands up her full height, making her lungs take a full breath. She doesn't need to be in such a hurry now, there is no one following.

Her feet on the soil tell her the stories of this place, impressions collected from all who have set foot on this path, familiar like the news of home. But she has no home anymore. That smooth trodden home-path came suddenly to a cliff. Now she is over the edge, falling.

She keeps to the tracks of the night animals, from bush to low tree, narrow, and she has to make herself small to pass by, scratched by the thorn shrubs and drooping branches. The small sharp pains remind her body of its size and mass, keep her from drifting up loose from the ground, giving weight to her feet so they can keep walking.

After a time the animal paths bring her to a cluster of large rocks. She edges between, into the space they enclose. Inside is a patch of sandy soil, its width twice her reach, its length slightly more. A nest where she can hide.

Hunger and cracked feet from the trail, hand still holding the knife, she slumps down and sits at the base of one of the boulders. Finally not moving, the feelings she had been outrunning start to catch up.

She folds her legs toward her chest, grips her shins, and rocks her head up and down, banging her forehead on her knees. Pain from thumping her head, it is too much and not enough.

She jumps to her feet and strides a circle inside the boulders.

"Aaaaaaaa," she howls, only a noise, not even a syllable, slapping her hand on rough sides of the rocks as she goes around.

All she was doing was following her days. The same as anyone, a woman keeping her place in her family. Help her mother spin and weave, collect firewood and carry water, listen to her uncles' stories. Isn't that what we have always done?

Then come these men with their weapons turning her whole world into violence and disgust. Weapons and threats, all force and aggression, why do they act that way, what pleasure do they get? Cursing as they eat, the nearest they have to friends are the men that they fight with.

Is that what they enjoy? Being masters of slaves? Where is the body pleasure in that? Is there some surge of power from bending people to their will? If it was really pleasure they were seeking, surely they could find some woman somewhere who would give herself freely. If they behaved like actual men instead of beasts.

Blood-lust and destruction, how can they choose that? In these last terrible months, she has been too close to those beast-men. She sees that they don't even enjoy the violence that they do.

Is it just blind compulsion? Or a reflex of anger, or an attempt to defend their status? And doesn't the violence just make them feel worse? It must be a strong habit, they don't seem to know anything besides inflicting more pain.

They laugh, they talk as if their sex is pleasure, but all she has seen is loathing — even of the men for themselves. Not just themselves, their disease spills out onto everything they touch. No wonder they are turning the land hard and dead. Their curse keeps them from knowing anything but their lusts, they destroy whatever gets near them. They have some kind of hunger that's turned around backward, like a lust for living, but for ruin instead.

They don't want life, they want power, and their only power is death. They are too stupid to see that they would gain more if they didn't fight. Too stupid or too fearful, afraid to unclench their fists.

But when they group together, those beast-men become stronger than real men. Following the king, or serving the king, or trying to be the king. Herd animals, most of them, asleep, yet still able to fight.

Real men cannot match them, not for long, they are too many. So much violence and waste to defeat them, how could a whole-man imagine it? And if he did, wouldn't he become a beast-man too?

Ninsigal's people love the world and killing repels them. When the beast-men kill, don't their bodies feel that revulsion too? But something has buried their natural reaction. Is it greed? Is it ignorance? Something bends their natural revulsion, making it push the wrong way.

She sees how it will be. They will devour the whole world. The longer she lives, the more ruin she will see. Ruin the land, ruin her family, ruin all that she loves.

Love? Does she even remember love? How to love after being covered with all that hate? And children? She won't let those beast-men have her children.

Their world is not fit for children. Living longer, dying now, or dying later, what difference could it make? Ending it now, all at once, what a relief that would be.

Why have a long dying that stretches out for years but ends with the same result? Let go of hope for living. Leave hope to those in her family who are strong enough to carry it.

She misses her family. She shudders at the thought of seeing them. Seeing how she is now. The thought wretches her stomach.

Her stomach is empty, with bitter bile at the back of her throat.

Use that man's metal of death. That man in Uruk was killing her, but he didn't finish. His knife was made for this.

The sun has gone down, far enough so the twilight has shrunk below the boulder horizon. A little less than half a moon is following the sun downward, bright against the dark. Not low enough yet to yellow, but hazy at the edges from the evening's moisture.

No more arguments, her anger releasing its heat at her forehead. She feels the ache at her temples, around the sockets of her eyes. Sourness deep between her hip bones and navel.

Dull ache of rib muscles when she breathes in. She jitters out of her dress and rolls it in a wad, sits down on the rocky sand and sets the dress-wad behind her. Sweet dark scent from the drizzle that re-wet last season's dry grass outside her rock nest.

Air moving silently stirring cool then warm, the smell of damp rock, the day's last warmth rising up to the night. Sitting still in the lull, she says, softly, "Hello jackal. I hear you there, quiet, stalking in the grass. Never mind that mouse, come here and take my body.

Bring your kin and feed your pups, my life will do you more good than it will me."

Holding her breath, she brings the knife to her forearm, pressing the vein. Metal sharp but insensible, lightly indenting her still living skin.

Press, gasp, exhale — she draws a deep cut. Her hand recoils and tosses the knife, she falls back on her dress pillow.

Blood on the sand for the ants and the beetles. Shiver, cold sweat, and nausea. Her vision tunnels to a triangle of stars directly above.

She hears the jackal sniffing the breeze, just before her senses draw together to a spot at her forehead, then fade.

— 16 —

It was at the full moon after winter solstice, only a few days after Gilgamesh made his triumphant return, that his mother, Ninsun took command of the temple of Inanna from the high priestess, Lilitu. But in the confusion before she was able to fully assert her power, some of Ninsun's enemies have dressed Lilitu in worker's clothing, smuggling her from the temple and out through the gates of Uruk. They take her on the road northward to Kish.

Lilitu meets with King Aga of Kish, and he meets with his ministers and then sends messengers to his allies in the nearby cities and temples. Among the many ministers and commanders and priests in the area surrounding Kish, there are an equal number of reasons for wanting to gather their armies together to take away some of Gilgamesh's swagger. After many more messengers and meetings and jugs of wine between the captains of the armies, it is almost the full moon after the spring equinox when Aga and his allies, together with a band of soldier-priests from the bull cult temples finally mass together at Kish.

They have assembled a large fighting force, all the men carrying spears, and the men carrying swords, and the bowmen with their arrows and shields, and wagons full of ground grain and dried meat and the supplies for the cooks, and all the donkeys to pull the wagons. They march southward to Uruk.

The donkeys strain at the wagons when they bog down on the muddy roads, and teams of men follow the wagons at the ready to push. Everything is wet, and it's hard to get a fire lit, but at least the sky isn't cloudy every day anymore, and the spring rain is not as cold as the winter rain.

As Uruk comes into view, the soldiers leave the donkeys and porters to their slow work and the soldiers quicken their pace. When they see the opposing soldiers on the city wall, they shout and raise their weapons and rush toward the gate. But before they can reach it, Gilgamesh's lookouts raise an alarm and the gate is bolted shut.

Now more of Gilgamesh's soldiers have mounted the wall, and they shoot arrows down at the advancing soldiers, and Aga's army pulls to a halt. Surely Aga can't be surprised that Gilgamesh got wind of his preparations for war.

It is clear to Aga and his captains that they are not going to finish this quickly, so they fall back beyond arrow-shot distance and order the combined armies to divide into groups, circling the city and pitching their camp tents a safe distance from each of the city gates.

Aga sets his main tent in the tender new grass of a low hill outside the north gate, with his commanders and foot soldiers and supply wagons spreading around behind him. The army at the east gate finds a low mound surrounded by drained marsh fields where they can pitch their tents away from the deepest of the mud.

To the south, the army has no choice but to camp in the mud. The men set makeshift tents on the donkey carts and huddle together when they aren't on watch. At the west of Uruk, the army makes their camp on the road across the river from the city. They plan to use boats they have taken from the ferrymen when it is time to advance on the city. They have surrounded Uruk and they settle into a siege.

— 17 —

Meanwhile, Enkidu is walking to Uruk to find Shamhat.

As Enkidu approaches Uruk, he sees the soldiers camped on the road to the city's west gate. They look like they are planning to stay for a while. In the distance, he sees smoke from another camp north of the city. Clearly, all these men are planning some kind of disaster. Why did he come here? This would be a good time to turn around and leave these soldiers to do their insanity without him.

He feels the knife parcel at his back. Did he come here only because of a knife? He imagines telling a story like this as a joke. Except this isn't funny.

He bends his path southward, following a farm track to start walking a great circle around the city, keeping his distance from the army camped against the western gate. Some of the farm fields are untended. Others have hastily made shelters beside the road where farmers are camping, stuck outside the city gates.

As he turns toward the river, he can see the army posted south of the city. The river has been swelling in the wet season, so he must swim across. The current carries him farther south before he reaches the far bank. The knife parcel swirls and bumps against his back and sides as he swims. But the cord doesn't slip off his shoulder.

He sloshes out of the river and through the reeds, shivering off the cold water. He walks on the high places when he can. He slogs through the marsh when he can't.

He sees the army camped in the mud, huddling around smoky fires, mired in, stuck doing nothing but waiting. Enkidu shakes his head, he's glad to keep moving, even trudging through the mud. Up ahead, as he makes his circle, he sees the army at the east gate. He finds a path around behind them. This army has a slightly better campsite but they look just as stuck. They seem almost as miserable as the army to the south.

Rounding his path to the northwest, the ground is a little higher. He has gotten behind Aga's main army and he sees the city's north gate beyond them. Uruk is surrounded. This would also be a good time to get away from here. The joke still isn't funny.

He keeps walking, exploring the low hills to the north of the city. The grass is greening, and a few shepherds tend their flocks of sheep. Not many farmers are in the fields, no doubt because of the war. Day after day he walks in circles, keeping an eye on the soldiers at their slow war.

There is no way into the city, soldiers are everywhere. Gilgamesh's on the walls and Aga's outside them, each relieving the boredom of their watch by yelling insults at the other side.

What is he even doing here? This isn't his home. He should just leave. What keeps pulling him to Uruk? Does he even care about these kings and their armies? Maybe they could all just kill each other. That would be an improvement.

Enkidu feels restless, but can't seem to turn away from Uruk.

How has he gotten tied up with the city? Clearly, nothing good can come from all these men here with their weapons.

He has many thoughts of Shamhat and still hasn't made sense of her. She was like two different women together in one body. Maybe more than two. Giving her complete attention to the power and politics of the temple, then moments later turning fully to the quiet movements of love.

He believed that he loved her. Maybe he still does. Is that why he is here: love? How does love fit in with all these soldiers?

After all that talk with Shamhat, did either of them really understand anything? True, their bodies had no doubts. He shivers at the memory of her body pressed against him.

It is early in the afternoon, and Enkidu has stopped on a small rise just west of Aga's camp. He is watching the soldiers around Uruk's north gate when he feels the air tighten, and then the ground begins to shake.

Gilgamesh's soldiers on the wall start shouting. Some of them run, some of them are frozen in confusion. There are clouds of dust rising up from the ground. Donkeys are running in every direction, crashing into Aga's men as they stumble around, confused.

Through the dust and disarray, a soldier from the bull cult army points and calls out that the earthquake has broken the city gates from their hinges. His brothers raise a shout and pick up their weapons. A crowd of Aga's soldiers rush with them toward the opening, finding their chance to finally break into the city. But Gilgamesh's soldiers are there behind the fallen gate, ready, and they slash at the attackers, cutting them down as fast as they come in.

Enkidu watches the armies push forward and fall back, swinging and chopping at each other in a tangle of blood and human limbs. He feels like he is about to laugh, but he can barely breathe. What could make any man do what those soldiers are doing? Running into the fray to get killed?

He watches them fight forward and back until it gets dark. Then the men who have survived trudge back to their camp, and it still doesn't make any sense. Sitting and watching the battle, he notices that he has dug his fingers into the damp soil at his sides, the tension in his hands gripping it tight. He takes a breath and loosens his fists, wiping his muddy fingers on his skirt.

In the morning Gilgamesh comes out of the gate with a retinue of soldiers and walks toward Aga's big tent. The two kings stand shouting distance from each other and argue, their soldiers lined up behind them with swords and spears at the ready.

Then one group of soldiers shouts all at once and runs at the opposite group, and then the others join in and they hack at each other, then fall back and run forward again for the rest of the morning. There is another lull, more shouting, and then more running skirmishes until the sun nears the western horizon when the fighting winds down again.

The armies face off across a small distance and they look like they are about to start shouting insults again when Aga hands his sword to his captain and walks up to Gilgamesh. All the soldiers crowd in a circle around the kings. Enkidu doesn't see anyone at the city gate.

It looks like this might be a chance. But does he really want to get into the city? And then what, in the middle of a war? What is drawing him toward the city? This would be another good time to get away from here. Why hasn't he just thrown the knife in the direction of the battle and gone home? Clearly, these people here are out of their minds.

He has spent days wandering around outside the city with the knife pressing on his back. Plenty of times he could have left already, but he hasn't done it. Is he just going to keep on walking in circles?

No one has moved on the battlefield. The kings are still huddled, and Enkidu doesn't hear any shouting. Evening shadows are stretching longer.

Enkidu sets off, circling wide behind the soldiers, crouching low until he is at the city wall, then skirting the base with his hand on the bricks until he traces around the massive door frame and steps over the fallen gate.

The street is empty, and he is just inside the wall. Then someone shouts an alarm and ten or twelve men spill out of houses from different directions and run toward him. Three men grab Enkidu. Some other men join them and they are all shouting and pushing him back out the gate.

Now there is more shouting coming from the crowd of soldiers out in the field. They have started fighting again. Some of the men crowding Enkidu run out to fight the army from Kish. Some of the soldiers come toward him from the battle. A pair the soldiers grab Enkidu from either side, pinning his arms behind him. Then there in front of him is Gilgamesh.

The whole of Gilgamesh's body is sticky with blood, thicker on the arms and legs, patches of dirt on his knees and blood speckling his face. Gilgamesh is twitchy and wild and hoarse. He shouts at Enkidu, "Who are you? What are you carrying? And why are you trying to sneak into my city?"

The soldiers holding Enkidu burn their fierce stares at either side of his head. One of them growls like a dog at his enemy.

Gilgamesh reaches out and yanks the braided grass cord from Enkidu's shoulder. He pulls the sheepskin packet out from between the soldiers holding Enkidu, rips it open, and sees the knife there inside.

A moment of confusion. Gilgamesh takes the knife in his hand and drops the sheepskin parcel. Disbelief. He holds the ivory handle. How can this be? Darkness begins creeping in at the edges of his vision. The hand holding the knife moves from side to side in front of him. Rage.

"What are you doing with a knife that has my first minister's mark on it? Are you the one who killed him? Was this because of that whore Shamhat?"

Gilgamesh looks down and sees Enkidu's skirt framed by the creeping darkness. "You stole that from me! What else have you taken?" Gilgamesh reaches out and slices the knot holding the skirt. It is stuck between the restraining soldiers. Gilgamesh yanks the skirt free and flings it aside.

The swing of his arm makes Gilgamesh even wilder. There is a rumbling sound coming up his throat. The shrinking center of his vision falls to the hairy dark place between Enkidu's legs. Gilgamesh grabs him, and slashing upward, hacks off Enkidu's genitals and throws them on the ground.

Enkidu cries out and the soldiers let him loose and Gilgamesh shoves him down. Gilgamesh steps over Enkidu bleeding on the ground. He stops a moment to tilt his head down and rub the back of his wrist across his forehead. The blackness is beginning to recede. Gilgamesh straightens, points to the clump of fresh gore flung in the dirt, and orders a soldier to pick it up. "Go take that dead meat to Shamhat the harlot."

Gilgamesh and the other soldiers go back to the massacre of the army from Kish.

⁂

Enkidu's vision starts to come back from behind the pain. He sees himself in the dirt in a war and with the dusk light almost gone. He needs to get away from here.

Rolling to his hands and knees, his fingers find the sheepskin with the sage that was wrapping the knife. He presses it between his legs and flinches at the pain. Maybe this will slow the bleeding. He climbs to his feet and stumbles through the gate in the direction of the temple.

Enkidu limps half bent over with his hand between his legs, an animal howl coming up his throat, each step catching him just before he falls. Halfway to the plaza he faints and collapses in the street.

In a mud brick house beside the roadway, a pair of women have heard the howling as it comes toward them, and they stand at their doorway looking to see what the noise is. They see Enkidu go down, and one of the women ducks back into the house.

She comes back out pulling the arm of a sleepy-looking man. The man fumbles to the side of the house and comes back with a short ladder, and the three of them tilt Enkidu into it and carry him to the doors of Anu where the priests take him in.

The priests wash him and bandage the bleeding. The wound is ragged and uneven, and they don't know what they can do about that. Enkidu has lost a lot of blood. Late that first night he wakes and the priests make him drink a big bowl of warm broth. Someone sends word to Shamhat, and she comes to see him early the next morning.

Shamhat is sitting next to his pallet when Enkidu's eyes open, her hand holding his. Enkidu's eyes say that he knows her, but his voice says nothing. Perhaps a flicker of a smile as he closes his eyes.

His wound is infected, and he drops in and out of fever dreams. Enkidu lingers four more days, his breathing getting more shallow, with a wet rasping sound.

⚏ ⊕ ◇

Shamhat came to visit him early in the morning on the day that he died. Perhaps his face twitched slightly when she kissed his forehead. She said, "Goodbye dear, I'm leaving Uruk. Some of the women will be coming with me to the temple of Ishtar at Ebla."

Gilgamesh has nominally won the war, but his army is ruined and the city is a shambles. After the fighting ended, another full day was consumed with shouting: Gilgamesh standing on one side with the few of his ministers that the messengers could find, and on the other side, Aga and his surviving chiefs.

The soldiers who were able to flee have all disappeared. Meanwhile, the wives and lovers and children of the killed soldiers are looking for bodies. They wail and hurl insults at both of the kings, along with anyone else who may have had any part in causing this disaster. Finally, Aga shakes his head in disgust, turns, and motions for his captains to come with him as he clumps away.

One of Gilgamesh's chief lieutenants has been killed, and his wife and sons follow Gilgamesh around, demanding that he give them land and cattle to pay for their loss. Soon the families of other dead soldiers, and some of the surviving soldiers, are crowding around Gilgamesh insisting that they be paid too.

Gilgamesh has been fighting and shouting for so many days that he can barely stand up, let alone speak, but he holds up his hands above the crowd and they quiet enough so that he can be heard.

He tells them that they have all contributed to the glory of Uruk, and the war is won because of their great sacrifice, and all the citizens will be forever grateful for what they have done in these last few days. They are heroes of Uruk.

The crowd remains silent for a few moments after he finishes his speech, and Gilgamesh manages a thin smile. Then the crowd starts shouting again and Gilgamesh loses patience, and with the last of his ragged voice he curses whoever gets near him.

It is the middle of the third day before enough of the shouting people get tired and start to leave, and Gilgamesh can drag himself back to the palace.

Everyone is gone.

He clumps up the steps to his room and falls onto his bed still covered in filth.

Another morning and he awakes.

The palace is silent, and when he calls no one answers. He is aching and dirty, he tumbles off his bed, trudging from one room to another.

There is no water. He is too young to be feeling this old.

He walks around the palace looking for something to eat. Hardened barley cakes, not picked up after some banquet. He gnaws at the barley, walking from room to room.

It would be nice to find some beer.

This latest war was really inconvenient, but at least he's won it, more or less. What a bad thing to follow the cedar forest adventure.

He'd been a hero, but now he's all alone and everybody's mad at him. As he shambles into the palace entry room, Gilgamesh spots a young man coming up the stairs outside the main door. The man is carrying something that looks like a pot of beer. Gilgamesh goes to meet the man outside the door, and motions for him to come closer.

The soldier's red skirt is stained from battle, but the man looks rested and bathed. He shifts his pot of beer to his left hand and thumps his right fist on his chest in salute to the king. Gilgamesh lifts his hand in response and says, "You'd be doing me a great service if you'd share me some of that beer." The soldier hands the pot to Gilgamesh, then follows him to where he sits on the stairstep in front of the palace.

Gilgamesh pats the spot beside him, and the young soldier sits. Gilgamesh takes a long drink from the pot, his eyes close as the beer soothes his throat. Finally setting the beer down on the step between them, Gilgamesh takes a long breath and looks over to the soldier.

"I think I remember you, did you come with me on the trip to the cedar forest? And you were here with me when we just beat that rabble from Kish too, weren't you?"

The soldier nods to both.

Gilgamesh tells him, "You're a good man. Even some of my captains didn't stick with me all the way to the end. Stay with me here at the palace, and when this is all sorted out, I'll find a good position for you." Gilgamesh picks up the beer and drinks, then hands it back to the soldier and he drinks too, sealing their deal.

It's a large pot of beer, and the men are becoming friends. The soldier has told Gilgamesh a couple of his stories from the trip to the forest, and he's laughed at Gilgamesh's boasts about all the trees that he cut. The sun is on their hair, warming them, and they are quieter now, not sure they want to bring up the slaughter of the war they just lived through.

The soldier turns to Gilgamesh and says, "I guess you really showed that wild man though, didn't you?"

Gilgamesh looks up. "What? What do you mean? What do you know about the wild man?"

The soldier says, "You know. When he came back here to betray you and you cut him down. But I heard that the priests at Anu got him and they kept him alive somehow."

Gilgamesh's body sways backward and he has to put his hands on the ground behind him to catch himself. He shakes his head, then heaves himself forward, breaking into a clumsy trot out of the palace grounds, leaving the young soldier sitting on the steps.

Gilgamesh is breathing too fast, and his head is floating with no thought, but his voice repeats "damn" as he runs across the city to Anu where he bangs on the door.

"It's me, Gilgamesh the king, and I need to see my friend the wild man."

The priest takes Gilgamesh's dagger and puts it on a table by the door, then leads him down a corridor to Enkidu's pallet.

The sun had been halfway from dawn to zenith when Gilgamesh got to the temple. Since that time he has been sitting beside the pallet with his hand on Enkidu's forearm. Only the small movement of Enkidu's ribs and the wet noise of his breath disturb the stillness of the room.

The sun has passed its zenith and moved halfway to the western horizon. And then there is only quiet.

Gilgamesh looks up with a jolt and listens. He doesn't hear another breath. He stands over the body, it still has Enkidu's face.

Gilgamesh climbs onto the pallet, grabs the body by its shoulders, and shakes. The body is still warm, the neck and shoulders flex, the head wobbles, eyes half open, like they might be looking at something, but clearly they don't see. Gilgamesh edges himself beside Enkidu on the pallet, picking up his nearest hand and lifting the arm around his shoulder.

He lays his head on Enkidu's chest, his ear to his heart. The heart makes no sound.

Holding the wild man's body, so much like his own, lying on his side on the pallet, Gilgamesh's muscles begin to release. He doesn't find rest, the missing heartbeat makes him lift his head.

Gilgamesh grabs Enkidu's beard at the cheek and takes a deep kiss at Enkidu's lips.

Gilgamesh unwraps himself from Enkidu's arm, slides off the pallet, and stands up. He wails and grieves, rocking forward and back, with his arms wrapped around himself. He rocks back too far and has to catch himself, turning to walk a circle around the pallet three times to the east then back three times to the west. He cries and staggers out of the temple, all the way down the streets of the city and out through the broken city gate still covered with blood.

He keeps walking with no thought to where he is going, beating his fist on his chest and howling himself hoarse all over again.

Night has fallen and Gilgamesh hasn't stopped walking. It is dark and he trips on a rock in the road. He is so exhausted that he sleeps right there with his face in the dirt.

In the morning he picks himself up again and keeps walking.

His tongue is stuck to the roof of his mouth. Maybe he's just been struck dumb for killing the only man who didn't want anything from him.

Is this some message from the gods?

In the end, didn't he love his friend Enkidu?

Did Enkidu ever love him?

Gilgamesh has no words.

Thus begins his year of wandering the roads between cities.

When his voice returns, he begins telling the tale of his friend the wild man.

Shamhat is loading a donkey cart for her trip to Ebla when her boy comes to tell her that Enkidu is dead.

The gossips at the city gates continue telling their stories.

They burnish them until they shine, and the stories start to say the things that people want to hear.

And the singers sing their songs about the hero Enkidu.

The end of
the end of
the middle.

FOUR

And so, Enkidu is dead. What was it exactly that killed him? Did he die of a curse from a god, or some random mishap, or was it a broken heart?

This all depends on who tells the story.

But we know how Enkidu's family died. They were crowded and starved and died from spear point or despair or some cattle-borne disease.

Do you see? Do you see where this is going?

Have you noticed how I've told this story?

No, I didn't tell it the old way. Not by the light of a campfire, in verse, from memory. But if I had, who would have been there to hear it?

And what kind of story would it be anyway, given the condition of my memory, and my faint powers of verse? That is why I am using these tools, these crutches, these prosthetics. Electric writing machines and their alphabets, attempting to rouse a human feeling.

We all belong to Gilgamesh now.

The beginning of
the beginning of
the end.

Afterword

The Epic of Gilgamesh is a remarkable tale.

It was written thousands of years ago when the foundations were still being set for the structure which we now call Western Civilization. The epic story contains gods and monsters and super-humans doing impossible deeds. It also has a character or two who are recognizable in the later Hebrew writings that got incorporated into still later Christian and Islamic texts.

Slightly less than 5,000 years after Gilgamesh, I am living in the United States of America. I don't recall exactly when I first read the epic, but I do remember why.

Sitting here with my computer screen in front of me, it is clear that something has gone wrong with Western Civilization. I had a feeling that this wrongness might have some roots deep in the past, and when I picked up Gilgamesh looking for clues, I wasn't disappointed. Gilgamesh comes off the page as incredibly modern. With only a small wardrobe change he would be right at home in the White House.

Interestingly, even today we still write stories with gods and monsters and super-humans. But I'm a product of a rationalist culture and not much a fan of super-hero stories. So when I attempted to understand Gilgamesh, I mentally dialed down the gods and monsters and super-human deeds, interpreting them as exaggerations to make a plot point more vivid. Then I tried to imagine an actual king in an actual Uruk doing big things somewhere around 2800 BCE. As I said, it wasn't difficult. Gilgamesh reminds me of people I know.

But I had a problem with Enkidu.

The relationship between Gilgamesh and Enkidu is central to the epic. The story would collapse without Enkidu. He enters as a vivid character, unique and powerful, and the narrative has to run to catch him.

But catch him it does. And then, after Gilgamesh and Enkidu have their colossal fight, Enkidu simply falls in line and becomes nothing more than Gilgamesh's loyal sidekick.

I don't believe it.

Enkidu is important. I believe that some of the wrongness we are experiencing these days in Western Civilization could be illuminated by the relationship between Gilgamesh and Enkidu.

Just as an example, isn't there a whole heaping pile of the Internet cobbled up from articles about wildness and masculinity and the abuse of government authority? Disagreeable as much of that writing is, surely it is evidence that many of our fellow citizens feel that there is something lacking.

I believe that a wild man could help us with some of those problems if only we could find an actual wild man, instead of yet another swindler dressed up in a wild man costume.

Anthropologists tell us that in our human past, there was a huge variety of ways people lived with each other and the land. Somehow we have lost the ability to imagine all but one or two of those ways.

We must also remember that when the Gilgamesh epic was set down on those clay tablets, it was to serve certain aims, to benefit certain authors. But perhaps when we read Gilgamesh we can still learn something from the clues that may linger in the margins.

The scribes doubtless had their biases and allegiances, which were certainly not in favor of any actual wild men. But still, those scribes were much closer to the culture and memory of the wild man than we are today. What if we look to see if any of the old culture lingers around the edges of the story?

What part of a wild man would a king need to alter in order to have him serve the king? What part of a wild man would a king want to preserve in order to reinforce his kingship?

Who were the people cast as heroes of the epic? Who supported the class of scribes that recorded the story?

Why did they feel the need to tame the wild man? Or was the wild man still wild, but hypnotized, or enslaved, or insane, or something?

What could possibly have caused Enkidu to act the way he does in the epic? Is it, as the epic asserts, because he simply loves Gilgamesh? That sounds like something Gilgamesh would say.

And isn't there something really similar in this story to what happened when Europeans met the natives of North America? How many times did the Europeans think the Native Americans were stupid or crazy when they tried to tell the Europeans what we now know to be the obvious truth?

Aren't we, even today, still misunderstanding people whose ethos is different than what grew out of Sumeria, Greece, Rome, and Western Europe? And isn't there ample evidence that much of the misunderstanding has been done willfully, for the capital gain of the people who then went on to write the history books?

Lately, though, it feels to me that the conflict goes deeper than simply stealing the land. The current era of Western Civilization seems to demand that we hold a certain set of approved beliefs in addition to just delivering our complicity. Isn't this much the same kind of emotional menace as Gilgamesh insisting that Enkidu loves him?

I've read the prefaces to a few translations of the epic, and I'll never come close to surpassing all those love letters to Gilgamesh in the canon. All the translators fawn over him.

But let's step back and look at one of the basic premises the epic sets for itself. The citizens of Uruk cry out and the gods hear them, and Enkidu is created to distract Gilgamesh from his tyrannical ways. But surely there is some other reason a manly man might stop raping virgin brides besides getting a hunky new drinking buddy?

All of Gilgamesh's commentators credit him with great wisdom, but isn't there some other way to get that wisdom besides his life-time of boorishness where he doesn't achieve wisdom until he is too old and tired to molest anyone anymore? (And don't get me started about masculine archetypes!)

This story is my attempt to break Enkidu free of Gilgamesh's world so he can be his own person, and so we can better look at the foundations upon which our world — Gilgamesh's world — was built, and see what else we can build instead.

ERIC FARNSWORTH

Eric Farnsworth isn't a writer.

He isn't much of a bicycle mechanic

or gardener or welder either, for that matter.

But still he does those things.

He and his wife Jean live in Kansas and dance tango.

SPHINX / SUL BOOKS

Sphinx is an imprint of Sul Books. Born from a collaboration of two long-time independent esoteric publishers, and named to honor the Suleviae — the sisterhood of goddesses revered at springs throughout Europe — Sul Books is dedicated to publishing works that manifest aspects of the sacred sight that heals what humans have harmed.

As with the thrice-fold kinship of the Suleviae goddesses, Sul Books combines the publishing strength of three resilient imprints: Sphinx Books, RITONA, and Gods&Radicals Press. Arising from these continuing legacies comes a fourth, committed to stand-out works of powerful transformation.

Find our other titles at Sulbooks.com